Tusk

Read more about Michael and Katya's adventures in:

SOS ADVENTURE

Tusk

COLIN BATEMAN

Hodder
Children's
Books

A division of Hachette Children's Books

For Matthew

A Catalogue record for this book is available from the British Library

ISBN-13: 978 0 340 99888 5

Typeset in AGaramond by Avon DataSet Ltd,
Bidford on Avon, Warwickshire

Printed and bound in Great Britain by
CPI Bookmarque Ltd, Croydon, Surrey

The paper and board used in this paperback by Hodder Children's Books
are natural recyclable products made from wood grown in
sustainable forests. The manufacturing processes conform to the
environmental regulations of the country of origin.

Hodder Children's Books
a division of Hachette Children's Books
338 Euston Road, London NW1 3BH
An Hachette UK company
www.hachette.co.uk

Prologue

London, England, 3 a.m.

PC Kevin Winters was mid-yawn when the stolen red Ferrari streaked through his field of vision.

119 miles per hour – in a 30mph zone.

It was going so fast that he might even have missed it, if he had blinked at the same time as yawning. His colleague, PC Jenny McFarlane, let out a surprised gasp and instinctively reached for the siren.

They didn't even have to speak. PC Winters gunned the patrol car out of the side road where they'd been parked, bored and waiting for the end of their shift, and took off in hot pursuit. The Ferrari was already disappearing from sight on a Fulham Palace Road slippery with rain. Adrenaline flushed through the young PC. He'd been on the force for two years, and ninety-nine per cent of his work was mind-numbingly boring. But challenges like this made it all worthwhile – a high speed chase, genuine danger, and the satisfaction of an arrest at the end.

Perfect.

As they roared after the sleek red car, PC McFarlane called in to report and to ask for support. They were required to do this – but were determined to have the vehicle stopped and the driver in handcuffs before any showed up.

It was going to be hard, though. The Ferrari was a high-powered supercar leaving a trail of destruction across central London. Wing mirrors were torn off parked cars as it sped past, tyres screeching. Red lights were ignored, crashes with oncoming vehicles narrowly avoided. Those few pedestrians still around at such a late hour leapt out of the way to save their lives. One cyclist hurtled into a parked taxi and went flying through the air.

'We're going to get ourselves killed,' PC McFarlane warned, her face pale, as they took yet another corner at speed.

'Not tonight,' said PC Winters, 'not tonight! He's

fast, but he's careless. We have to stop him before he kills someone!'

As word spread across the police network, a tried and trusted plan swung into action. Very soon a helicopter was tracking the pursuit and relaying pictures back to HQ. Streets and junctions were blocked off as the Ferrari was channelled towards Green Park and the Mall, where an ambush would be set: two chains of spikes spread across the ground and only raised as it approached, puncturing its tyres and causing the driver to lose control. It was a wide expanse of road in the midst of a public park that was likely to be devoid of other traffic, parked vehicles and most importantly, late night revellers.

As the plan roared towards its climax, PCs Winters and McFarlane buzzed with excitement, knowing they would be first on the scene when control was yanked out from under the Ferrari.

'Steady . . . steady . . .' PC Winters said under his breath. 'Calm . . . calm . . .'

Then finally the Ferrari skidded onto the long, straight, tree-lined Mall, deserted as they had hoped; at the far end stood Buckingham Palace itself, still regally lit, with its gates shut tight, and all other exits already blocked.

This was it, the end of the pursuit.

Three quarters of the way up the Mall, the two lines of spikes were suddenly raised, and in a fraction of a second all four tyres were shredded. The vehicle lurched to the left, then back to the right, went up on two wheels, toppled over and then slid on its roof in a straight line for nearly thirty metres until finally coming to a halt and bursting into flames right in front of the Palace.

PC Winters's patrol car was the first to reach the crash. It skidded to a halt and both of them leapt out. PC McFarlane had a small fire extinguisher which she immediately began spraying, while PC Winters crouched down beside the smashed side window, reached inside, released the seat-belt holding the driver upside down, and dragged the idiot out.

Other patrol cars arrived, and very soon there were two dozen cops surrounding the burning car, not to mention the security teams who had swarmed anxiously out of the palace.

And they all stood looking in amazement as the driver stood up.

Not more than fourteen years old.

Cocky.

Unapologetic.

'What seems to be the problem, officers?' the kid purred, raising a thumb towards the now open gates of the palace. 'I'm just parking outside my house.'

Chapter One

Michael Monroe didn't *think* he was in heaven, he knew he was there.

It was possibly the softest and most comfortable bed he had ever slept in.

He had no way of knowing if he had been out cold for one hour or twenty-four. All he was sure of was that he had enjoyed one of those hugely satisfying dreams where everything – and he couldn't remember quite what – had worked out well, and now he had woken to the first rays of sunshine, squeezing through the wooden slats that served as his bedroom window, feeling gloriously warm, totally refreshed and absolutely up for anything. The soft whirr of the ceiling fan was soothing, the rotation of its blades hypnotic, and he lay there groggily, knowing that he could easily drift away again, but determined not to. There was too much to do, too much to find out. The SOS Artists, of whom he now counted himself a fully-fledged member, even if they did not quite, had arrived in darkness last night, knowing only that they were landing at a farm belonging to Dr Kincaid, their organization's founder, situated in the heart of the Zambeziland savannah. The few questions he had managed to ask – *Why are we here? Why does Dr Kincaid have a farm? What emergency are we being plunged straight into?* – had been roundly ignored by everyone.

There was a light knock on his door. Before he could respond, it opened a few inches and a man in a white waiter's jacket grinned at him. 'Excuse me, sir, breakfast?'

'Yes, absolutely.'

The door opened fully. The man stood to one side to allow two of his colleagues to enter before him. Each was carrying an immaculately carved wooden tray. As Michael sat up in bed, one tray was placed across his lap, the other at his side.

'Sir,' said the first man, 'this morning we have freshly squeezed orange juice, melon, banana, bacon, scrambled eggs, toast, raspberry preserve and pains au chocolat. And on *this* tray we have fried eggs, sausages, hot chocolate, croissants, grapefruit juice and strawberries. Is there enough here for you, sir, or would you like to order something else?'

'No, no, this will be just . . . fine,' said Michael.

In the boarding school, before he ran away to join SOS, breakfast had consisted of oats that tasted like a cross between sawdust and budgie food.

'And will that be all, sir?'

Michael almost said, 'No, could I have a slap in the face to wake me up? I think I'm dreaming.'

The men quietly exited. Before the door was fully shut, Michael *attacked*. He was starving. He wanted to gobble it all up before he was snapped suddenly out of the dream. He was probably really lying in a swampy trench somewhere chewing on a mouthful of ants and suffering from a rare and life-threatening tropical fever. But the more he ate the more he realized that the food before him was very real, and in so realizing he forced himself to slow down so that he could truly savour what had been placed before him. It was *delicious*. The scrambled eggs were so soft, so immaculately prepared, that he imagined they came from a hen that had been pampered for all of her life.

When he had finished – and he ate *all* of it – Michael set the trays to one side, threw back the quilt, stood up and stretched. He padded across the floor – thick with exotic rugs – and pulled open the two wooden, slatted doors. He didn't quite know what he expected to see. He knew he was on a farm, so quite possibly there would be some kind of African cow, skinny ones with big horns, perhaps tended by tall warriors in scarlet robes or half-naked women who carried pots of water on their head. He had *no idea*.

But what he did see was . . . stunning.

A vast, epic, panorama was laid out before him; a lush, verdant pasture sweeping down to a river shimmering in the early morning sun. And on the near bank and shallows of that river: elephants. Further in: rhinos. On the other side, loping along: giraffes. It was as if someone had painted a picture featuring everything they had ever imagined about African wildlife, squeezing it all into something that was utterly unrealistic, and then stepped back and uttered some ancient incantation which magically brought it all to life. It was all there before him.

Michael stepped out onto the veranda, placed his hands on the top of the wooden fence, and blew air out of his cheeks. The sun was still low in the sky, but hot already. Twenty-four hours before he had been in New Guinea, with its clawing, sticky, unpleasant heat, but *this* felt wonderfully invigorating, as if it was breathing life into his tired batteries.

'It's incredible, isn't it?'

Michael turned to his right. Katya, his teenage comrade and occasional enemy in SOS, was standing in exactly the same position on her own veranda.

'It's . . . magical,' said Michael.

Katya pointed. 'Oh, look!'

They watched as a flock of pink flamingos glided in to land gracefully on the water, not disturbed at all by the crocodile whose snout was clearly visible just a few feet away. It was as if the giant reptile was ignoring them because he was too busy enjoying a nice swim, and was thinking he couldn't be bothered eating them because he was on holiday.

'When Dr Kincaid said he had a farm,' said Michael, 'this isn't quite what I imagined.'

'I knew he had a place in Africa, but nothing like this. It's amazing. We should go exploring.'

'Absolutely.'

She was smiling across at him. Usually they fought like cat and dog, but perhaps, Michael thought, the luxury of their new surroundings and a good night's sleep was helping to mellow her combativeness. Michael smiled back.

Katya smiled some more.

Michael was starting to find it unnerving. A smiling Katya was rare enough, but grinning like an idiot for such an extended period was grounds for an examination of her mental faculties.

'*What?*' Michael finally demanded.

'If we're going exploring – you'd probably want to put some clothes on?'

Michael's mouth dropped open at exactly the same moment that realization dawned. He was absolutely and completely naked.

As he thundered back into his room, his hands covering the bits he had to cover, he could hear Katya cackling like a hyena.

It was like a cross between a hunting lodge, a mansion and a holiday resort. Almost the first thing they found was a swimming pool, complete with slides. It was attended by three men whose sole task appeared to be fishing out any bugs that happened to land in the water. The water was crystal clear and, when they dipped their toes in it, beautifully, refreshingly cold. They had both just agreed to jump in in their underwear when they were approached by another white-jacketed member of staff. They were being summoned to see Dr Kincaid.

As they walked, the man said, 'This is your first time in Zambeziland?'

'First time in Africa,' said Michael.

'It is very beautiful, no?' the man replied. Michael nodded. 'This farm, every direction, for one hundred kilometres, owned by Dr Kincaid. He very important man.'

'We know,' said Katya.

They were led back into a lounge that was open to the elements on two sides. The Artists were sitting around, chatting and drinking coffee: Dr Faustus, their medical expert, was engaged in earnest conversation with Bonsoir, who was in charge of planning and supplies, and was their linguistics expert. Bailey, their pilot, had a pair of binoculars raised and was watching the wildlife down by the river. Mr Crown, the muscles of the outfit, a fearsome warrior and adversary – fearsome *colleague*, for that matter – was sitting on a bar-stool, quite happily shaping a piece of wood with a very large knife. Dr Kincaid had a mobile phone clamped to his ear, and nodded at Michael and Katya as they entered. It was unusual for Michael to see the Artists like this – so relaxed. Normally, wherever they were, you would also find banks of television screens reporting the world's trouble spots and natural disasters, and dozens of computers showing dangerous weather patterns or simulations of approaching hurricanes; there would be multiple phone lines manned by SOS staff urgently discussing supply lines or refuelling or interrogating locals half a world away about civil wars or government oppression. But *here*, there was scarcely anything in the room that would have looked out of place in an African hunting lodge a hundred years previously.

Dr Kincaid closed the phone and sat on the edge of the large snooker table that filled one corner of the room. He was wearing khaki shorts, sandals, a white T-shirt, SOS baseball cap and Armani shades. He didn't say anything, but everyone fell silent. He nodded around them slowly. 'Guys,' he said, 'it's been a long year, a dangerous year – but I know you wouldn't have it any other way.'

'I would,' said Bailey.

Everyone laughed.

'That's because all you do is fly around in your little bird,' said Mr Crown, 'while we do all the dangerous stuff.'

'Whatever you say, Big Man,' Bailey replied, 'but next time you're surrounded and call on me to get you out of there, I'm turning a blind eye and a deaf ear.'

'Which is exactly how you fly,' said Mr Crown.

'OK,' said Dr Kincaid, holding up his hand for quiet, 'what I'm saying is it's been tough, particularly these past few weeks, and we could all do with recharging our batteries. *This* then, is a little thank you from me. For the next two weeks our Artists in the US and in the Far East can deal with whatever comes up, because you lot are officially here on holiday. You will be waited on hand and foot, the finest chefs in the world will prepare exactly what you want to eat, you can lounge by the pool, use the state of the art gym, you can go off on safari or use my library and watch any movie you care to name in my private cinema. Just do whatever makes you happy, it's a gift from me to you.'

They broke into spontaneous applause.

Michael grinned at Katya.

And then Dr Kincaid went and spoiled it all by adding: 'That is, except for you two.' He pointed at Michael first, then Katya. 'You're going on a mission. You can enjoy your holiday when you return. I mean, *if* you return.'

It took about three seconds to sink in.

And then Michael *exploded*.

Dr Kincaid, the adult Artists, and of course, Katya

herself, knew exactly how volatile he could be. Michael certainly knew himself what he was like, and did his best to control his flare-ups, but this time, *this* time he was being pushed too far.

'That's just not fair!' he roared. 'We've worked every bit as hard as the rest of you, we saved the Eden satellite, we rescued Dr Roper from inside a volcano, we've risked our lives repeatedly and now . . . and now . . . you're sending us off on some . . .'

Michael's words trailed off, finally aware that it wasn't particularly cool for him to blow his top, that everyone was looking at him, and that he didn't quite know what to say next.

'Do you want me to explain why you're going on this mission in private?' Dr Kincaid asked, his voice calm, 'or do you want me to do it in front of everyone?'

'I don't . . . *care*.'

Dr Kincaid looked at Katya. 'What about you?'

'Whatever way you want to tell us.'

Katya always played her cards close to her chest. She was naturally patient, but also had enough experience to know that there was a reason for most things, and she needed to find out what it was before she came to her conclusion. Only then would she explode, if required. She was aware that Michael was staring at her.

'*What?*'

'Aren't you going to stand up for yourself?'

'Michael . . .'

'Forget it!'

'Michael?' This time it was Dr Kincaid.

'What?!'

'Calm down.'

He glared at Dr Kincaid. Then took a deep breath.

'It's not fair,' he said, his voice quieter.

'Michael, you, and Katya also, have done well since you joined us. Yes, you recovered the Eden satellite, and of course, my sister would not be alive without the pair of you. But good fortune has also played a large part in your success, good fortune which could easily have become bad fortune. You have disobeyed direct commands and repeatedly put yourself in harm's way. We cannot allow that to continue. The journey you are about to embark on will instil in both of you the importance of following orders, the importance of team work, and it will hone your survival skills. In short, it will turn you into better SOS Artists. You will be joining up with Major Calvin Hunter, an ex-commando, a hunter, a survival expert, the best on this whole continent. He's leading a group of teenagers who have each been selected because they are suffering from various behavioural problems – from having criminal convictions to drug addictions; mixed-up, fragile, aggressive kids, you name it, they've got it. You will take nothing beyond the bare essentials with you, no phones, no laptop, no GPS, no internet; you will walk until you can't walk any further, you will sleep under the stars, and survive on your wits. There are creatures out there that want to eat you. If you get as far as Mount Zambella, the second highest mountain in Africa, you will then climb it. You haven't been with us long, Michael, but this will definitely be the toughest thing you've ever done.'

Michael was still glaring. Katya's mind was working overtime. They both spoke at the same time.

'It's a *punishment*,' said Michael.

'It's not a *mission*,' said Katya.

'It's a *trek*,' said Michael, 'like tourists do.'

Dr Kincaid smiled ruefully. 'No, it's not a punishment. It's just another step along the path to becoming a fully-fledged Artist. And yes, it's a trek, but it's the *Star Trek* of treks. A lot of it will be to where no man has gone before. And as for it not being a mission? Well, actually, yes it is.'

'To go for a *walk*?' snapped Michael.

'No, Michael, the primary purpose of your *mission* is to provide security for one of your fellow travellers. A fourteen-year-old tearaway called Peter Windsor. Your job is to stop him somehow killing himself, or anyone else for that matter, and to make sure he returns home safe.'

'And why exactly are we doing this?' Katya asked.

'Because Peter Windsor just might one day become the King of England.'

Chapter Two

They were in the back of an open-topped truck, rattling along a deeply rutted track. Their vehicle must have had suspension at one point, perhaps back in the 1960s when it was built, but it had long since lost it. Now every time they plunged into a pot hole the entire vehicle and every single one of their bones shuddered and threatened to snap.

It was an hour since the reason for their trek had been revealed, and Michael had just about settled down. Sixty minutes in which more details of their mission had been given, equipment had been gathered and farewells exchanged. The other Artists didn't seem unduly upset to see them go. They were too busy jumping in and out of the swimming pool, drinking cocktails and generally having a good time.

Michael was somewhat embarrassed by his lack of

control, but still felt hard done by. They had worked just as hard as the other Artists, and the reason the Eden had been recovered and Dr Roper saved was precisely because they had disobeyed orders. Making them rigidly obey commands might improve their discipline, but at what cost? He also believed that Dr Kincaid had deliberately set him up, knowing he would overreact and thus proving the wisdom of sending him on the trek. If their boss had handled it differently then they might have jumped at the opportunity and the challenge – what wasn't there to like about walking through some of the most beautiful country in the world, the chance to track and observe all kinds of wildlife, to camp under the stars – and, to top it all, to climb the second highest peak in Africa? And all in the company of not just a legendary hunter but also a real-life Royal?

When he said to Katya, between bone-crushing bumps, that Dr Kincaid was just as much to blame for his bad-tempered outburst as he was, she shook her head and called him an idiot.

He was used to this by now, and didn't react, beyond asking why.

'Because you don't know him at all! He's always testing you. He says things the wrong way round not to make you lose your temper, but to teach you a lesson. Do you think that when he's meeting world leaders, presidents, kings, people who are starving or who have lost loved ones, and every one of them is demanding that SOS does something *right now*, or are threatening him or screaming in his face, do you think he can afford to lose his temper and explode the way you did?'

'Uhm, no?'

Katya sighed. 'Exactly.'

'I'm not an idiot.'

'Well, you do a very good impression of one sometimes.'

'You're here with me, so he must think you're one as well.'

'No, I'm here to keep an eye on you.'

'Yeah, that's right.'

She made a face. He made one back. They both looked in different directions. And they both smiled. It was, very much, business as usual.

While they packed for their trek, Dr Kincaid had hovered; his earlier abruptness had evaporated, and he had become anxious to impart as much advice as he could. He seemed genuinely worried about the task ahead of them. He kept muttering, 'There's no back-up . . . there's no back-up . . . and I'm not joking. No back-up. If there's trouble, you'll have to get yourselves out of it. Did I say there was no back-up? We won't be hiding in the bushes watching you. We won't be hovering overhead or slipping electronic trackers into your shoes.'

He had paced behind them some more before launching into it again.

'This is about discipline and doing what you're told. Your task is to protect the Prince above all else, and that includes your own personal safety. And you can't let him know who you are. If he thinks for one second that you're there to guard him, he'll walk out. He knows he has to do this, but he has to do it on his own terms.'

'Isn't it a bit risky, sending possibly the next King of England out into the middle of nowhere?' Katya asked. 'Especially if we're not allowed GPS or phones?'

'Absolutely,' was Dr Kincaid's sober response. 'But his father is quite insistent. He would rather have his son be eaten by lions than allow an idiot to ascend the throne.'

'Is he an *actual* idiot?' Katya asked.

'Well,' said Dr Kincaid, 'it's a matter of opinion. He seems to believe that the laws of the land don't apply to him. Trouble with a capital T.'

'But his father knows about us, right?' Michael asked. 'He knows there's some extra protection besides Major Hunter, even if you don't think we're up to much.'

Dr Kincaid shook his head and smiled. 'He hasn't a clue. And I wouldn't be sending you if I didn't think you were up to it. You're doing very well with SOS, I just think you can do even better.'

It was, Michael thought, *exactly* what was called a back-handed compliment.

'So if his father doesn't know about it, who is sending us?'

'I am. And some influential friends. It's a little extra insurance. You've a long trip in front of you to even get to the camp. Use it to think about your back-story – you need to come up with credible reasons for you being there so you won't look out of place with five equally troubled kids.'

'Just make something up?' Michael had asked.

'Yes. But something about an unfortunate background, the scrapes you've gotten into – something serious enough to have you sent on the trek. This has to be your last chance or you'll be sent to a Young Offenders Centre.'

Katya nodded at Michael. 'He doesn't have to make anything up, he's got exactly that background already.'

He would have snapped something back, if she hadn't been completely right. Instead he said, 'What about you, Princess Tippy-toes, what's your story going to be?'

'Orphaned by war, sold into child slavery, kidnapped by a madman, rescued after six months and haven't recovered from it yet.'

'Is *any* of that remotely true?'

'You'll never know.'

But there was something about the way she looked when she said it that told him there might be some inkling of truth in it. He hadn't thought much about the circumstances that had brought her to SOS. There had to be something in her past life that explained why she was such a pain in the neck to be around. Maybe the trek would actually do her some good.

One thing was perfectly clear – their driver, a rotund, smiley guy in ragged trousers and a dirty red T-shirt, had little time for the finer points of the Highway Code. Or even the general principles. He just pointed the vehicle in the direction he wanted it to go, and drove towards it irrespective of what was in his way. He took up a position in the middle of the track, and kept to it. For long stretches the saw grass on either side stood more than six feet high, effectively making it seem like they were driving through a tunnel. The track also twisted and turned, with so many corners they often couldn't see what was coming towards them. This did not noticeably inhibit their driver from racing around them as fast as he possibly could. Michael saw more than a dozen people hurl themselves out from under the wheels of the truck and into the surrounding saw grass at the last possible moment and, as they disappeared completely into the vegetation, he had no idea if any of them emerged unscathed or, indeed, alive.

It finally got the better of Katya. She leant forward and yelled at the driver through the back window of the cabin. 'You're driving like a maniac!'

'This is Africa!' he shouted back, grinning widely. 'Everyone drives like a maniac!'

And he did not slow by one single mph. They roared through a small village, with rickety wooden stalls set up on either side of the road, and tended by women in brightly coloured skirts and tops. The stalls were filled with fresh fruit and vegetables, and huge cuts of meat surrounded by clouds of flies. There were warm bottles of Coke and packets of batteries. The women yelled at the driver to stop and buy, and he responded by honking his horn and covering the women and their goods for sale alike in a cloud of red clay dust.

Three hours later, tired, sunburned and suffering from what Michael described as *numb-bum-itis*, their driver finally slowed down and veered off the track on to an even narrower, more overgrown one. He rumbled into and out of its even deeper potholes for a further ten minutes, before pulling into a clearing where they could see two other trucks, a group of kids roughly their own age and a man in a green khaki top and shorts, wearing a black baseball cap and mirrored sunglasses. This had to be Major Calvin Hunter, their team leader.

Michael pulled his rucksack up and jumped down. He quickly ran his eye over the other kids, trying to pick out which one was royalty. Two girls – he could count them out. Three boys. The only thing they all had in common was that they looked unhappy to be there. None of the three looked particularly impressive. None looked as if a crown might sit easily on his head.

Before he could properly decide which of them was

the most likely candidate, Major Hunter barked, 'You're late!'

'We came as soon as—' Michael began.

'Quiet! The time to speak is when I ask you to speak.'

'Sorry, I—'

'Quiet! We operate under strict discipline here. Any talk back will be severely punished!'

'But I didn't mean to—'

'OK, have it your own way! It's going to be dark soon – your job is to erect all of the tents before it is. Understood?'

Michael *almost* spoke. He just managed to hold his tongue, and forced himself to nod instead. He suddenly realized that the one question neither he nor Katya had asked was whether Major Hunter was in on their secret. Was he starting out mean because he knew, and didn't want to show any favouritism, or did he not know at all and he was just mean to start with? Indeed, did he even know that the Prince was actually a Prince?

Katya landed on the grass beside him with her rucksack. 'Good start,' she whispered.

'And *you*!' Major Hunter shouted. 'No talking! You were late as well. You can make the fire and cook the supper.'

Katya looked astonished. 'Me? But—'

'And tomorrow night as well!'

Katya took a deep breath. Now that he studied them more closely, Michael saw that the other kids were looking just as shell-shocked as he and Katya were. Their rucksacks lay up-ended before them, their contents spilled and obviously picked through.

'Before you get started,' Major Hunter barked, 'let's see if you've broken any more rules. You knew them before you got here. So empty that rucksack.'

He was pointing at Michael. Michael obliged. He unzipped the top and emptied out his sleeping bag, a wash bag, a change of clothes and a flashlight. Major Hunter crossed to him, kicked open the sleeping bag, nodded, then lifted the rucksack and peered inside. Next he felt the pockets on either side, found something, unzipped one, and produced a spare set of batteries. He threw them down on the ground with the rest of Michael's gear, but didn't otherwise comment. He moved along to Katya.

'Now you.'

Katya hesitated for just a moment before pulling out her sleeping bag and wash bag, her change of clothes and her flashlight and then set the rucksack at her feet.

Hunter picked it up and weighed it in his hand. He raised an eyebrow.

Katya started to say something, but thought better of it.

Major Hunter turned the rucksack upside down – and out fell a notebook computer and a mobile phone.

Katya swallowed.

'Is that it?' Hunter asked.

Katya nodded.

Hunter felt the zipped pockets, and stopped on one. He opened it and produced what Michael recognized as a mini-GPS device.

Katya looked surprised. He dropped the device and then brought his heel down hard on it, grinding and smashing it into the hard ground.

He stood before her, the sun reflecting off his shades, his eyes impossible to read – but there was absolutely no doubt about his feelings towards Katya.

'Anything to say?'

'I—'

'Anything to say?'

'I must have—'

'ANYTHING TO SAY?!!'

The penny finally dropped.

'Sorry,' Katya said.

'I don't hear you!'

'SORRY!'

'That's more like it. What's your name?'

'Katya.'

'OK, Katya, you took a chance, and you were caught out. To compound it, you lied about the GPS. You, madam, are on latrine duty. Do you know what that means?' Katya nodded. 'Well, in case any of you don't, in case any of you have led such pampered, spoiled lives that you have no idea what a latrine is, it's a toilet, it's a hole in the ground that has to be dug every day so that you can pee and poo into it. Someone needs to be responsible for digging it, and then filling it in when everyone is finished. It is the most degrading and disgusting job in the whole camp, and it's all yours, Katya, understood?'

'Understood.' Her eyes were almost bulging out of her head with the effort of keeping her temper at bay.

Michael on the other hand – well, it was all he could do to keep himself from bursting out laughing. He wasn't sure if he'd ever been happier.

Chapter Three

They built up a sweat unloading supplies from the trucks, which then promptly disappeared, leaving them alone in the bush. Michael set about pitching the tents, Katya was dispatched to dig the latrine, and the others were instructed to collect firewood. They were all given a stern warning to watch out for snakes and poisonous spiders. They worked steadily, not venturing too far from camp, and always under the watchful eye of Major Hunter – at least, they thought they were under his watchful eye. He was leaning back against a tree, with his rifle across his lap, but with his reflective sunglasses it was impossible to tell if he was watching out for them or sleeping.

Michael and Katya's paths only crossed once during the afternoon, as they both paused momentarily to have a drink.

'Enjoying yourself?' Michael asked.

'Shut up, you're an idiot.'

'I know I am. It was idiotic to plant that GPS in your rucksack.' He winked and moved on.

She stood open mouthed, before suddenly spitting: 'I will have my revenge.'

'Yeah, yeah, whatever. Keep digging that poo hole.'

Major Hunter, perhaps alerted by their conversation, roused himself from his tree and sauntered across to where Katya had dug the latrine. She wiped an arm against her dank brow and said, 'I think I'm done.'

He nodded and said, 'That is the perfect latrine.'

She smiled. 'Thanks, I—'

'Except it's too close to camp. Dig another one, about twenty metres further out.'

He turned on his heel. Katya looked daggers after him. Then she saw Michael giving her the thumbs up out of the corner of her eye, and transferred her glare of doom to him. Major Hunter then inspected the tents Michael had thus far erected; he said nothing, but quickly returned to his tree. Michael took it as tacit approval.

Darkness came suddenly. It was almost as if someone had switched the lights off. Their encampment became a whole different world. The cries of animals and birds, the buzz and flap of the insects; they must have all been there in daylight, but at night they seemed to be ridiculously amplified, or worse – closer. The fire they built was impressively large, and they made sure there was plenty of spare wood to keep it going. Katya, to her credit, proved an able cook, frying steaks and rice which they devoured. Left to their own devices they would probably all have gotten to know each other, but Major Hunter's constant presence was intimidating, particularly as he failed to remove his sunglasses, and the flames reflected in them made him look like a devil. As they ate he said, 'Enjoy it, from here on in we're on basic rations.'

When they'd finished, they washed their plates and utensils with a thoroughness Michael suspected that none of them – apart perhaps from Katya – would have shown at home. When they were done they returned to sit around the fire. It wasn't just because the night had cooled considerably, or for the protection it offered. There was something powerful about sitting there, in the middle of Africa, far from what they considered to be civilisation, having cooked their own food, with the stars above them as brilliant as they had ever seen them. They all seemed to feel it. Words were not required.

But Major Hunter provided them anyway.

'I'm not going to give you guys any bull,' he said, his voice deep, gruff. 'You all know why you're here, and that this is going to be tough. Very tough. But I'll tell you something. You're all going to make it. If one of you flops out, we all flop out. This is about teamwork, one for all and all for one. There's an old saying – *know your enemy*. But it's much better to know your friend, your comrade, because that's what you are or will become. You have to be able to trust each other. You have to be able to depend on each other. You must not only know each other's strengths, but also their weaknesses. *You . . .*' He pointed suddenly at a surly looking boy with shoulder length dyed blond hair, with his black roots showing badly. 'What's your name, why are you here, and what do you hope to gain from it?'

He looked a little shocked to be singled out. 'Jake,' he said quickly.

'Jake what?'

'Ahm, Jake McDonald.'

'Why are you here?'

'Well, it's a long story.'

'Shorten it.'

'Oh. Well. I ran away from home.' He shrugged.

'What you mean is, you ran away from home twenty times, you broke into a number of houses and stole money to support yourself. You got into a fight with police who tried to arrest you, but you were out of your head on whisky, and injured two of them before you were subdued.'

Jake looked a little shell-shocked. 'Ahm, yes,' he said.

'And what do you hope to achieve here?'

'Ahm, a new start?' he suggested.

'Honestly?'

'Ahm, yes. And, well, I also hope to avoid going to prison.'

Hunter nodded. Then he pointed at the girl beside Jake. She had a goth look about her: black hair with a pink streak through it, eyeliner, a tattoo on one arm, several earrings, a nose stud, and dark clothes appropriate for the street but not the bush. 'You next.'

'Sam. Samantha if you must. Sam Bourne. I've been in a Young Offenders Centre, and broke out. I actually do want a new start.'

'You weren't just in the YOC for drugs, were you?'

'OK. No. I stole a car. I sold a lot of my parents

furniture when they went away for the weekend to pay for my drugs.' She shrugged.

The next to fall under the spotlight was a tall, thin boy with a pale complexion and his hair cut short.

'Pete,' he said. 'Peter. Peter Windsor.' He spoke with a fake Cockney accent. He was trying to come on like he was working class and not the Prince he was. 'I got into a bit of bother, bit of thieving, rich houses, expensive motors, got caught, didn't I? You pick on rich people, you get a longer sentence. I got offered this lark by Social Services, anything's better than being banged up inside, so here I am.'

'You think it's a lark?'

'A camping holiday and a stroll in the jungle suits me just fine.'

He grinned around the campfire. Nobody returned it. Michael suspected they were all thinking the same thing: Pete was just a bit too cocky, and it was bound to get him, and by extension all of them, into trouble.

Major Hunter studied the Prince for a long time, and then moved to the next boy, a heavily built kid of Indian extraction.

'Ash,' he said, 'Ashley Khan. I've done nothing wrong, my parents just want me to lose a bit of weight, get fitter.'

'So burning down that mosque has nothing to do with it?'

'That was an accident.'

'And the second time?'

'I was framed. It was an electrical fault.'

Major Hunter kept his flaming lenses steady on Ash for fully twenty seconds. Ash stared at the fire. The girl beside him ended the awkward silence by saying, 'I am Petra Ilych Petrovska. I am a child of Russian immigrants. My parents say I have deep-set emotional problems. When I'm upset, I cut myself, and sometimes when I'm not upset too.' She offered up her arms for inspection. They were criss-crossed with scars, some ragged, some straight and fine. 'What do I want to get out of this? Dunno really. I wasn't given a choice.'

Major Hunter's head moved ever so slightly, the flames on his glasses becoming even more apparent as his angle to the fire changed, to settle on Katya.

'You two arrived together, and are late additions to the group, so I don't have your paperwork and don't know your background. However, I would suggest that you are scrupulously honest, because if you lie to me I will find out, and will deal with it appropriately. Katya, isn't it?'

'Katya, yes. Katya Nijinski.' Michael knew that

surname was a lie to start with. 'I was caught up in an earthquake when I was on holiday with my family in the Middle East. I lost my parents and two brothers. This was eighteen months ago. I haven't been back to school since.' She paused then. She shook her head. 'No, that's a lie. I did go back to school, for one week. I was expelled. For fighting. I put two guys in hospital.'

Michael smiled to himself. She was making them think she was tough so that they would be reluctant to mess with her.

'I suppose I just want to learn to enjoy life again.' She smiled hopefully around the campfire.

'Very good,' said Major Hunter. He turned to Michael. 'Now what about you?'

Remember why you're here, don't say anything smart, don't cause trouble, stick to your story.

'Michael Monroe.'

Good start. But then it all went rapidly downhill. He couldn't help himself.

'Sorry to disappoint you all, but I've never been in trouble and I've no unfortunate history. I'm part of the Action Response Team working with SOS – you know, we're the guys who fly into the world's danger zones and save people. I'm here to brush up on my survival and leadership skills. Also, I intend to be the first up that mountain we're heading for, so I guess I'll see you all up there.'

Chapter Four

Michael had gambled. He figured that if he stuck to the truth, even if he wasn't believed, then he could never be caught out in a lie. He expected a short-term punishment, with the possibility of a long-term gain. What he got was a long-term punishment and no prospect at all of any gain. A gamble, indeed. One that had failed. Major Hunter gave him three chances to tell the 'truth', and then condemned him to stand guard duty that night. He also relieved Katya of latrine duty and gave it to him instead – for the rest of their trek.

'Nice one,' Katya said, under her breath.

'What a plonker,' added Pete Windsor.

'Let me tell you about something that happened a couple of years ago,' Major Hunter said. 'I had a guy like you, been nowhere, done nothing, but thought he knew everything. I made him guard for the night, but soon as everyone had gone to sleep he thought he could nod off as well, nobody would know any different. While he slept, a lion came into camp, entered one of the tents, got a kid by the throat, so he couldn't scream, and dragged him away. We eventually found him the next afternoon. Well, we found part of him. Do you get what I'm saying?'

Michael returned his steady look. 'I won't fall asleep.'

Major Hunter nodded. 'But—'

'*What?*'

'I'm weapons trained. Anything comes near camp I'm going to need your rifle to scare it off or kill it.'

Major Hunter smiled. 'I don't think so.'

'Well, what am I supposed to do?'

'I have the perfect weapon for you, *Michael*. If you think you're man enough to handle it.'

'Should be.'

The Major stood. Everyone watched as he stepped across to where they'd stacked their battered metal plates to dry in the heat from the fire. He lifted two and carried them back to his original position and sat down.

'If you see a lion, Michael, you take this . . .' He raised one of the plates. 'And you batter it against the other like this . . .' He clanged them together. 'And then you run towards the lion, repeating the action. And if you want, you can shout, *Shoo! Shoo!* at the same time.'

Everyone laughed.

Everyone except Michael.

And Major Hunter.

And the laughter quickly faded when they realized he was serious, and that all that stood between them and getting eaten alive by a lion was an idiot who had nothing more than two plates to bash together; and that he mightn't even have them if he was fast asleep.

Michael had stood guard before – very recently. In New Guinea he had allowed sleep to overtake him, put the entire mission at risk and been punished for it. He had sworn that he would never put himself or SOS in that position again.

He was on edge for the whole night. There was just something different about being in the African bush compared to the rainforests of New Guinea. Although there were thousands of potentially lethal insects and poisonous snakes in that part of the world, here there were not only insects and snakes, there were also huge animals that could tear you limb from limb. Big cats that spent their lives hunting, that could sneak up and pounce and you wouldn't have a clue. And he was certain something was moving out there. The way the dark outline of a bush seemed to move in the opposite direction to the way the slight breeze should have been pushing it; the way he seemed to hear *purring*. Sometimes he was sure it was so close that he could almost smell its dusty flanks and matted mane, and then a fly would buzz past his ear and he would almost collapse with fright. To make matters worse, Major Hunter, the survival expert, hadn't given him any instructions at all, other than his demonstration with the plates. Was he supposed to stay in one place or patrol the camp? Was it safer to stay close to the fire for protection, or would the fire act like a magnet, drawing all kinds of creatures in? He ended up doing a little of everything: staying still, then hurrying around the camp perimeter; standing in the firelight, then crouching in the dark. Major Hunter didn't come to check on him once. He had warned him he wouldn't. Instead, he said he would just count heads in the morning to see if anyone had been dragged off and eaten. None of his new companions came to offer moral support. Even Katya, his comrade and occasional friend, didn't offer her expert opinion or try to wind him up.

He was alone.

Totally alone.

Everything would have been fine, he was sure, if only he had a rifle with night vision and a telescopic sight.

But instead he had two plates with which to defend himself and the camp.

It was a very long night. He was alternatively drenched in hot and cold sweats. There was absolutely no chance of him drifting off to sleep. He kept the fire fed. He patrolled. His eyes grew used to the dark. He kept telling himself: you're with SOS, you're an Artist, you have faced down a polar bear, confronted wolves and survived a volcano, you should not be jumping out of your skin every time you hear a twig snap.

Eventually, after something like fifty years had passed, there was finally, finally a hint of grey on the horizon, and his heart soared. His night shift, his night*mare* would soon be over.

The grey gradually spread; there was the hint of a rising sun, an orange glow that leant an interesting tint to the mist hanging over the savannah. Michael surveyed his surroundings. He saw the first signs of movement from the camp. He had clambered up into the lower branches of a tree – partly because it gave him a better view of the surrounding scrub and partly because he didn't think rhinos could climb – when Major Hunter emerged from his tent, stretched and yawned, and then began to walk slowly towards where Katya had dug the latrines. His head disappeared behind the bushes, but then unexpectedly reappeared further along from where Michael knew the latrines were. He grinned to himself. Major Hunter was too important to use the communal toilet, he was off to create his own. As he disappeared behind some trees Michael slipped off his branch. He was desperately tired now, but knew better than to try and get some sleep without being officially relieved of guard duty. Just because it was now fully light didn't mean that the danger had diminished.

He knew that some people took forever to go to the toilet, but when there was still no sign of Hunter returning after ten minutes, Michael was overcome with curiosity. He slipped off his branch and padded through the camp. He gave the latrine a wide berth and cautiously approached the edge of the trees. He had no wish to catch their leader with his pants down, so he cleared his throat several times, loudly. When there was no response, he ventured under their canopy. Within a few metres he discovered that the trees were set along the top of a slight incline. He found himself looking down at a fairly narrow channel peppered with boulders. He guessed it was a dried-out river bed. Major Hunter was perched on one of the larger rocks. The first rays of the sun were reflecting off a metal flask he was raising to his mouth. Michael knew immediately that it was too small for water – but perfect for hard liquor.

Well, well – drinking before breakfast!

He didn't know if he was delighted to find a chink in the Major's armour, or disappointed. Probably a bit of both. What did it mean? And what to do with this information, this discovery, this potential weakness?

Nothing yet.

There was no need to tell anyone, not even Katya, but he would store it away, knowing that he had it to use next time Major Hunter picked on him.

Michael, quietly satisfied, was just about to turn back to camp when he was suddenly drawn to movement on the far bank of the barren river, perhaps about forty metres from him and twenty from where Major Hunter was taking another mouthful.

A lion.

A *lion*.

Michael's heart leapt into his mouth. Major Hunter

was facing in exactly that direction, but it was impossible to tell if he had spotted the big cat. And it was *big*. A male, with a huge bristling crown of a mane, sleek and fully grown, his ribs clearly visible, but more like the equivalent of a human six pack than an indication of weakness or starvation. The lion padded down the low bank and began to circle the rock. Major Hunter – did not move a muscle. Was he playing it cool, or had he drifted off into a drunken stupor?

He has no rifle.

Ohgodohgodohgodohgod . . .

The Major's rifle had seemed like an extension of his body. He was supposed to be the big survival expert – and now here he was face to face with a lion, and no means of protection. Michael didn't know whether he should shout a warning which might cause the lion to attack or keep absolutely silent and hope that it was just curious. If he did shout, it might attract the lion to *him*, or the camp beyond. He didn't even have his plates with him.

Finally, Major Hunter's head moved. He was awake and aware. But was that an improvement – knowing that a lion was about to tear you to shreds?

Michael knew he could shoot and kill the lion if he

could get the rifle – but it would take a couple of minutes to race back to Hunter's tent, and the same to get back. It was too long, too far.

Do something.

Do something!!!!!!!!!

DO SOMETHING!!!!!!!!!

The lion was closer, closer . . .

Michael was about to shout, but even in those few moments between the decision being made and any sound erupting, the situation changed dramatically. Major Hunter gently lowered himself off the rock and stood upright facing the beast. The lion stopped its padding. A low growl travelled effortlessly across the still cool early morning air. The ridiculous thing was that Michael couldn't tell if it came from the lion – or from Major Hunter.

What was he *doing*?! Was it some trick he had learned after years in the jungle? Stand up to your attacker, show him you're not scared? From where Michael stood that seemed like utter madness.

But it wasn't. Because what Major Hunter did next *really* was. It was the stupidest, most moronic, insane thing he'd ever seen.

And quite possibly the bravest.

Instead of the lion attacking this lone, defenceless

and quite possibly drunk man – this lone, defenceless and quite possibly drunk man attacked the lion.

Major Hunter *charged* at it.

He wasn't trying to scare it off, he was *taking it on*. He hurled himself upon the creature. Before it could fully open its jaws or swipe at him with his lethal, jagged paws, Major Hunter had it by the neck and had wrestled it to the ground. Michael had a sudden optimistic thought that the Major might have a knife in his boot and could ram home this sudden and unexpected advantage, but no, all he had was his hands, and the King of the Beasts would not be subdued by them alone; he was stronger than any man; he fought back. In moments the two of them were rolling around the river bed amidst sickening roars and cries and throwing up a cloud of dust that partially obscured them.

Michael knew he was already too late to save Major Hunter. But he also knew what he had to do. The lion was a man-eater. Once it had a taste of human flesh everyone in the camp would be at risk. He had to kill it. Michael dragged himself away from the slaughter and hurtled back through the trees, past the latrines and into the still sleeping camp. He threw himself into Major Hunter's tent, grabbed the rifle, and sped back to the river bed, checking it was loaded as he ran.

All quiet.

He had been gone . . . three minutes, max.

No roars, no screams. With the rifle raised to his shoulder Michael inched down the incline towards the rock. He roved the sight around the river bed, his finger already tight on the trigger, trying to figure out where the dripping jaws of the big cat were, where the torn limbs and bloody carcass of their leader lay.

Michael's whole body was shaking. He took a deep breath, steadied himself, and slowly rotated 360 degrees, convinced that the lion was about to throw itself upon him from the trees, from the river bank, from the surrounding saw grass, but . . . *nothing*. Sweat cascaded down his brow, his T-shirt was dripping. Michael ventured forward . . . *There* in the dust, paw prints, boot prints, evidence that the creature and the hunter had embraced in a terrible dance of death. But no blood . . . no flesh or bone or gristle. The lion had done what Major Hunter had told them about that night by the campfire, he had dragged his victim away somewhere else to eat, or maybe to share with the rest of his pride.

What to do? What to do?

Instinctively, Michael moved back towards the

camp, emerging from the trees and surveying first the latrines and then the tents. Nothing moving. As he approached, one flap opened and Katya emerged. She was swigging from a bottle of water, but stopped as she saw Michael, the rifle raised and the look of terror on his face.

'*Michael?*'

He ignored her. He continued to scope the tents. He moved in behind and around them. He checked the surrounding tall grass as far as he dared.

'Michael? What is it?'

One by one the others began to groggily emerge, only vaguely aware at first that something wasn't right, hardly even registering that Michael was armed until their heads had cleared sufficiently to ask what he was doing with Hunter's rifle.

'Hunter's dead,' said Michael. He continued to move the rifle around the camp.

'You . . . you shot Hunter?' asked Jake, his blonde hair mad from sleep.

Michael glanced around at them. Their immediate reaction was the same: that he might actually have done it. Michael returned his eye to the sight.

'A lion got him. Out there. He went out without his rifle.'

They were exchanging glances, unsure whether to believe him.

Katya moved closer, and Michael jolted at the unexpected movement and brought the gun around on her. She stopped.

'Michael . . . it's OK.'

'It's not OK,' said Michael, 'he's dead.' His face was drained of all its colour, his eyes were bulging out of their sockets, his voice incredulous and tremulous. 'I've never seen anything like it . . . he fought it, fought it, but it was no use. He's gone . . . it's just us now.' His eyes fell on Peter Windsor. 'Don't worry. I swear to God, I *am* SOS. Katya too. We're going to protect you, protect all of you. We'll get you out of here.'

Katya was just about to speak – but he would never find out if it was in support of him, or if, even now, she intended to keep up her charade of being just another troubled kid. As her mouth opened, a shout came from the other side of the camp.

'YOU!'

Michael spun, his finger on the trigger, the sight zeroing in on . . .

Major Hunter, striding towards him, his shades on, every limb in its proper place, and not a sign of blood anywhere except in the language he was about to use:

'WHAT THE BLOODY HELL ARE YOU DOING
WITH MY RIFLE? PUT IT DOWN BEFORE YOU
KILL SOMEONE!'

Chapter Five

The little group of troublemakers struck camp and was on the move by 7 a.m. Major Hunter had not yet indicated what Michael's punishment would be for scaring his companions with a blatantly ridiculous story about his being eaten by a lion, nor for potentially putting them all in danger by stealing his rifle. Michael, for his part, was just too confused and amazed to put up any kind of argument or protest. He was really, *really* thrown by Major Hunter's sudden return. It made *no sense*. He knew what he had seen, the horror and shock of it would stay with him for ever. There was *no way* that Hunter could still be alive, let alone unmarked by his tussle with the king of the jungle. And yet there he was, striding ahead of the single column of trekkers, absolutely fit, perfectly confident, no map required. He had issued his instructions just before they set off: 'Don't wander, keep hydrated, don't drink it all at once; if you have a problem don't suffer in silence, let someone know; keep your eyes peeled for imaginary lions.'

They walked for three hours straight, and the cool of the morning soon gave way to an intense sun. They were all creamed up, but still they burned. Michael was fatigued from his guard duty and lack of sleep and stayed at the back. But he didn't mind the physical aspect. He knew he was tough enough to keep going for days. It was the mental turmoil. He just couldn't work out what was going on. Had he imagined it? Hallucinated? Maybe he *had* fallen asleep and had a brutally realistic nightmare? Or what if he'd been bitten by an insect and suffered some kind of psychotic reaction? Or what about his new companions? Weren't they all criminals and drug addicts? Michael glanced over at Sam, Samantha Bourne, the goth. Hadn't she already admitted her drug problems? What if she'd slipped him something? What if . . .

'See enough?'

In examining her, he had also inadvertently caught up with her, and now she was glaring at him.

'Sorry, what?'

'You were staring at me. What's your problem?'

'No, nothing, I was just—'

'Fancy me, do you?'

'No! I mean, what are you talking about?'

'Don't believe you. Don't believe anything you say. At least we know why you're really here now. Liar, liar, pants on fire, yeah? Some kind of mental condition, yeah? Nutter, yeah?'

'Takes one to know one,' said Michael, instantly aware that it made him sound about eight years old.

'Grow up,' Sam hissed.

'Yeah, right,' Michael snapped back. 'And nice nose ring!' he shouted after her as she marched ahead of him.

Katya dropped back. 'Nice one,' she said, 'you're doing just great. First, you nearly screw things up with your SOS story, now this bull about a lion attack. *Are you unwell?*'

'Yes. Yes I am. I'm sick of all this crap. I know what I saw.'

'You think you know what you saw.'

'*No*, I *know* what I saw. I just can't explain it. Yet.'

'Michael, I don't know what's got in to you, but you better sort it out. We're here to do a job, if you can't . . .'

She stopped. Pete Windsor had crouched down to tie his boot lace.

As they passed him he hissed, 'Watch out for them lions.' And then added, 'Plonker.'

Michael took a deep breath. 'I think I was drugged,' he said quietly.

Katya studied him as she walked. 'Michael, *why* would anyone do that?'

'I don't know. But considering our company, maybe just for badness.'

Katya didn't comment. She didn't need to. The way she rolled her eyes and moved on said it all.

When they eventually stopped for the night, Katya began to set the fire and prepare a meal of chicken and rice. Pete Windsor knelt beside her and smiled. 'You should let Ash do the fire – he's the expert.'

He had probably meant it to be funny, but Katya just looked at him. Ash, on the other hand, was close enough to overhear and immediately snapped out: 'What did you say?'

'Nothin'.'

'I heard you.'

'Then why are you asking? Deaf as well as fat?'

Ash smiled. 'I've heard them all before. Sticks and stones.'

'Sticks and stones what?'

'You've never heard sticks and stones? Sticks and stones will break my bones but names will never hurt me. It's an old . . . like, a nursery rhyme? For example, I could call you a thieving little cockney swine, and you wouldn't need to take offence.'

'Really?'

'Really, you thieving little cockney swine.'

Pete nodded. Then he threw a punch at Ash's nose. Ash, clearly expecting it, leant expertly back and then brought up a left hook under Pete's jaw that sent him reeling back. Ash hurled himself after Pete, forcing him down and began beating him around the head. Pete was thin, but wiry and strong, and he bucked under the assault, trying to throw Ash over his head; but Ash was too big and it only half worked, and he ended up sitting on Pete's face. They were all sucked into it, shouting for one fighter or the other, or shouting at both of them to stop it. Katya, obviously, tried to end it by dragging them apart, and got an elbow in the nose for her efforts. She spun away, ran the back of her hand under her nostrils, saw a few drops of blood, then glared at Major Hunter, who was watching it all with complete detachment.

'Aren't you going to *do* something?!' she yelled at him.

Though it was quickly getting dark, Major Hunter

still had his shades on. He shook his head slowly. 'Out here,' he growled, 'it's survival of the fittest.' And after several moments, punctuated by yells of pain from Pete as his arm was twisted back and his left ear bitten, Major Hunter added, 'And sometimes, survival of the fattest.'

Katya looked at him incredulously. He was supposed to be looking after them and yet he was just standing there allowing them to kick and punch and tear lumps out of each other. She spun towards Michael.

'Stop them, Michael!'

'Stop what? Is there a fight? Are you sure you're not imagining it?'

He grinned at the fury on her face. He glanced at Major Hunter, wondering if this was all part of his plan, if he was allowing them to fight as some bizarre way of working out the pecking order in their group. Wasn't that how wild animals did it? From deer to wolves to lions? As Michael's eyes met those reflective sunglasses, he thought he saw a smile cross the Major's lips, but it was so fleeting that he wasn't completely sure it was there in the first place.

As the boys continued to roll around and their energy and determination showed no signs of flagging,

Major Hunter lazily stretched before lifting his rifle, raised it to his shoulder and aimed at the fighters. His finger curled around the trigger.

Katya was starting to say, 'What are you—?' when Major Hunter pulled the trigger and the rifle bucked back against his shoulder. The explosion finally rolled apart and cowered down. It was the surprise of it, the noise so loud against the comparatively quiet background. Invisible birds flapped panicking out of trees, and somewhere in the far distance they heard the bugle of an elephant.

Major Hunter lowered the rifle before striding across to stand over Pete and Ash. 'You fight like girls,' he snapped. 'No dinner for anyone tonight. Now get those tents up.'

He turned and walked off to sort out his own.

Jake, Sam, Petra, Katya and Michael stood in shock. Ash and Pete looked at each other, and shook their heads.

'Is he serious?' Pete hissed.

'You are both *idiots*!' Petra shouted.

Pete got to his feet. He ignored Petra and glared after Major Hunter. 'It was only a bit of a scrap,' he said.

The others gave him disgusted looks and began to

drift off to organize their tents. Michael stood over Ash, who was still on the ground, and put his hand out to give him a pull up.

'I don't need your help!' Ash spat, and then got up, although not without some difficulty and a lot of puffing. He began to dust himself down, and then his brow furrowed, and his hand went to the back of his neck and touched it gingerly. When he withdrew it, Michael saw that it was wet with blood. Ash looked at Michael in disbelief.

'He . . . shot me! He only bloody shot me!'

'No . . . it must have been Pete.'

Michael moved behind Ash, pushed his head gently forward so that he could get a proper look. There was a very straight, very narrow slice along the back of his neck. He was absolutely certain that it hadn't been caused by the boys tearing at each other. It was too perfectly formed. It didn't look dangerous or deep, and there really wasn't that much blood.

But still.

Michael came back round, nodding. 'It grazed you. It's not too bad.'

'He *shot* me.'

Michael stood looking towards where Major Hunter's tent was already almost up. He nodded. 'He did. He definitely shot you.' He turned back to Ash. 'Go and see Katya, she'll have band aids.'

'But . . . but . . . what are we going to *do*? He shot me! That's not right, that can't be right! Is everyone on this trip mad? If my father knew . . .'

'He will.' Michael put a calming hand on his shoulder. 'But there's nothing we can do right now. OK? Just go and get it sorted.'

Ash blew air out of his cheeks, before nodding and walking slowly, muttering away to himself, towards Katya's tent, taking care to give Major Hunter's as wide a berth as possible.

Michael stood where he was, watching Major Hunter work quickly and methodically. He knew the purpose of the trek was to give these troubled kids an experience that might knock some sense into them so that they might emerge as better, more rounded human beings. But out here, in the middle of the bush, surrounded by wildlife that could kill them and natural conditions and terrain that were extremely difficult and dangerous, they were very much innocents abroad. They were depending on one man, one expert, to pull them through. A man who had already survived wrestling with a lion, who was a secret drinker, and who had now shot one of his own charges

– either by accident or design. What had Ash asked him? *Is everyone on this trip mad?*

Michael shook his head.

No, everyone on this trip wasn't mad.

Maybe just one of them.

Chapter Six

'This isn't what I had in mind when he said we were going to be relaxing for a few days,' Bailey moaned, pulling at the bow tie around his neck. He felt like he was being strangled by it.

'We tried relaxing,' said Mr Crown. 'Didn't work.'

'Well, this isn't any better.'

It was true. The Artists had enjoyed all the luxuries that Dr Kincaid's magnificent African retreat provided – for about twenty-four hours. They'd eaten the gourmet food, swam in the pool, lain on sunbeds and enjoyed massages and working out in the state of the art gym. But they were men well used to action and adventure, it defined them, and switching off was hard.

What they actually wanted was trouble. Somewhere in the world there was bound to be something to test them. Somewhere they could provide their expertise, somewhere they could save lives. What they didn't want was to be dressed in formal jackets and trousers, sipping cocktails at the British High Commission in Zambroula, the capital of Zambeziland.

It was a comparatively prosperous country. Its money came from diamonds, minerals and oil. It had once been part of the British Empire, and still retained a healthy population of ex-pats who enjoyed not only the wonderful weather but the largely stable environment: so many other African states were rife with civil war and corruption. Zambeziland was largely peaceful, and its government was less corrupt than most.

As in most African countries, the money belonged mostly to the ruling elite, and the ordinary people missed out. That was why Dr Kincaid was such a popular figure – he used his considerable influence to fight on behalf of poorly paid diamond miners, to make sure that the oil companies did not damage the environment, and generally kept a watchful eye on the politicians and the generals to make sure that freedom of speech was defended and rights were upheld. This event at the High Commission was packed – everyone was there to celebrate Dr Kincaid's return to the country. It was described locally as the social event of the year.

Indeed, Bailey was beginning to thaw out a little – as one of the celebrated SOS Artists, he had a certain attraction to women. After consuming several glasses of Champagne, he happily regaled an admiring group of them with tales of derring-do, always making sure never to make himself into the hero of the story, while also making sure that secretly they actually believed he was. He was very good at it and had his eager fan club eating out of the palm of his hand – at least until they were suddenly distracted by an excited, red-faced man appearing in the open veranda doors of the palatial room where the party was being held and shouting 'Fight!' before disappearing outside again.

Immediately *everyone*, including the stuffy High Commissioner himself, flocked outside into the brilliantly lit gardens where two very large men were busy trying to kill each other.

One, Bailey saw, was Mr Crown. He had his jacket off, his sleeves rolled up, his muscles were bulging through his bloodstained and sweat-soaked shirt front – but his bow tie was still perfectly in place. The other guy was also in a formal suit that clung to him, emphasizing his heavily muscled torso. He had a tough, angular face, and shoulder-length, sun-bleached blonde hair. As Bailey watched, Mr Crown whacked the stranger across the side of his face, and he went down. A moment later he was back on his feet – and *smiling*. Then it was his turn. He brought up a wonderful left hook, and Mr Crown went flying. And then *he* was back on his feet and throwing another punch. The crowd *oohhd* and *ahhhd*. It was like watching an arcade game of two mighty warriors forever locked in combat.

As Mr Crown got back to his feet, he hissed, 'Yes, it is,' through bloodied teeth.

Each time the other guy hauled himself up he shook his head and said, 'No, it isn't.'

Bailey spotted Bonsoir, and moved up beside him. 'What are they fighting about?'

Without taking his eyes off the struggle Bonsoir said, 'The capital of Peru.'

'*What*?'

'Mr Crown thinks it's Lima, the other chap doesn't.'

'And that's why they're . . . ? But Lima *is* the capital of Peru. *Isn't* it?'

'Yup.'

'So why are they still . . . ?'

'Cos the other guy won't believe him, and Mr Crown won't admit he's wrong.'

'But he's right.'

'Exactly. Though I think that even if he *was* wrong, he wouldn't admit it. Sometimes he likes to fight. And win.'

'He always wins,' said Bailey.

'Always,' agreed Bonsoir.

'Maybe someone should tell the other guy that.'

'After you,' said Bonsoir.

The fighting continued. Their arms grew tired, their faces progressively more disfigured, but neither was inclined to stop – at least until Dr Kincaid, distracted by an important phone call, pushed his way through to see what all the fuss was about, and saw what punishment his toughest employee was taking – and giving out. Immediately he did something nobody else was prepared to do. He stepped between them.

'Please – what's this all about? I'm sure we can sort it out!' He had twenty years experience of chairing peace talks between warring states. 'Now come on, why the fisticuffs?'

By saying *fisticuffs* he made it sound as if they were being very childish.

'It's about him admitting he's wrong,' said Mr Crown, through swollen lips.

'No,' said the other guy, 'soon as *you* admit *you're* wrong.'

'About what, precisely?' asked Dr Kincaid.

'The capital of Peru,' said Mr Crown.

'Lima?' said Dr Kincaid.

The blonde guy's eyes narrowed. 'I'm not falling for that. You two guys are connected.'

Before Dr Kincaid could respond, the High Commissioner finally did something worthy of his post. He stepped up beside Dr Kincaid and said, 'As a matter of fact, before I was sent here, I worked in the High Commission in Peru, and I can absolutely confirm that Lima is the capital.'

The blonde guy said, 'You're serious?'

'I'm always serious,' said the High Commissioner, with a conviction that suggested he was.

'Oh,' said the blonde guy. 'Well. Looks like I was wrong then. Has been known.' He gave a little bow towards Mr Crown. 'You sir, you are one of the toughest men I have ever punched.'

Mr Crown returned it. 'Likewise,' he growled.

'Now that's settled,' the blonde man asked, 'mind if I buy you a drink?'

'I'll buy you one.'

'No, I insist.'

'No, *I* insist.'

Dr Kincaid raised a hand. 'No, *I* insist . . .'

Mr Crown and the blonde guy examined each other, then nodded in unison.

'Well, thank goodness for that,' said Dr Kincaid.

Mr Crown stepped towards the blonde man, with his hand extended. 'Name's Crown, I'm with SOS.'

'Never heard of SOS,' said the blonde guy, taking the hand and squeezing it firmly. Mr Crown squeezed just as firmly back. 'Guess I spend too much time in the bush. But if they're all as tough as you, next time I pick a fight I'm going to make sure I know what I'm talking about. Pleased to meet you. The name's Hunter, but most people call me Major.'

Chapter Seven

For three days and nights, Michael watched Major Hunter like a hawk. Or, more appropriately, given their location, like a vulture. They were *trekking*, not *walking*, and it was hard work. But it also felt good. Always in the distance was snow-capped Mount Zambella, their ultimate goal. Without the proper instruments there was no way of judging how far away it was. Some days when they made good progress it seemed closer, almost as if they could reach out and touch it. At other times it felt like they could walk for ever and get no closer.

Michael shrugged off his fatigue and enjoyed the challenge. He did what he was told, he wasn't cheeky, he did his best to get on with his companions – but all the time he was examining everything their leader did with forensic intensity. Was the Major mad or just a bit strange? Maybe living on your wits in the wilds of Africa did that to you.

The others were coping with the challenges of their journey in different ways. The goth, Sam, seemed to enjoy going out of her way to wind Michael up, but he actually quite liked her. Katya didn't understand her at all. She didn't get her look, her multiple piercings, her sense of humour – particularly her humour, which was odd, because it was very close to Katya's own: biting and sarcastic. She was also just as certain that she was right all the time. The girl of Russian extraction, Petra, was suffering worst with the sun, her very pale skin was mostly covered, but where it had been exposed she was burned raw. Heavyweight Ash worked hard and wasn't puffing or complaining quite so much. He made a point of staying well clear of Major Hunter. Jake was just the opposite, always right behind him – even attempting conversations with their leader, although they never went anywhere. Jake was ruddy with health and having a ball. In fact, they were all beginning to get along a little better – with the exception of Peter Windsor, who seemed to be rubbing everyone up the wrong way. Katya said to Michael, quietly, that they should make an exception for him – it couldn't be easy being brought up as a Prince, with everyone waiting on you hand and foot. Michael thought just the opposite – it sounded *really* easy. He should try living on a tough housing estate and running the gauntlet of drug-crazed gangs every day if he wanted to know what wasn't easy.

'And have you ever lived on a housing estate with drug-crazed gangs?' Katya asked.

'No,' Michael conceded, 'but my butler told me all about it.'

She made a face. He made one back.

Michael didn't know if Major Hunter had forgotten his punishment, or if, in light of Ash and Pete's fighting, he had decided to transfer it to the group as a whole, but the work duties were now evenly divided up between them – whether it was erecting the tents, digging the latrines, preparing the fire, cooking the food or standing guard overnight, everyone did their fair share, and mostly without complaint. Only Pete Windsor had something smart to say. When they made camp on their second night and he was instructed to organize the toilet, he pointed at Michael and said, 'I thought it was supposed to be his job.'

'No,' Major Hunter said crisply, 'it's yours for tonight. And tomorrow night.'

'*And* tomorrow . . . ?'

'And the next night.'

Pete just about stopped himself from responding. The message was understood and he kept his mouth shut. It didn't stop him throwing a filthy look in Michael's direction.

Whether Major Hunter was slowly giving them more responsibility, or he had realized the folly of arming a night watchman with just two plates (not that three would have helped), when it came to Katya's turn to stand guard, he instructed her in the use of the rifle. Katya nodded along, and fumbled it a little bit the first time she raised it to her shoulder. Michael knew she was an expert in most weapons, and that this was purely for show.

'I'm giving you one bullet,' said Major Hunter. 'Otherwise you'll start shooting at everything that moves, including branches and birds. If you have to shoot, make sure you know what you're shooting at, because you won't get a second chance.'

Katya just nodded innocently.

Before she began her shift, Michael, who had hardly spoken to her since they'd begun their trek, came up beside her and said quietly, 'You OK, one bullet?'

She nodded. 'It's enough.'

'What if there are two lions?'

'I'll take them both down with one.'

'I think you probably would. Stay safe.'

'Are you being sarcastic?'

'Yes, I really want you eaten by lions, or a giraffe.'

'Now that *was* sarcasm.'

'Nope. Especially about the giraffe. It would be a long, slow death.'

She rolled her eyes and told him to go to bed.

There were no disturbances during the night, but when he saw her the next morning she looked hollow-eyed and pale.

'Long night?'

'Yep.'

She discharged the single bullet from the rifle and handed it back to Major Hunter, who took it without comment. The next night, Jake was given the same short lesson in the use of the weapon and issued with his bullet. They retired to their tents soon after. Within twenty minutes the relative peace of the African night was shattered by the retort of the rifle and Jake backing into camp wide-eyed and shaken. As they swarmed around him he gasped out: 'There was something out there . . . I shot at it . . . I don't know if I hit it . . . There was something out there . . .'

'What was it?' Sam asked.

'I don't know!'

'Did it roar or . . . ?' asked Petra.

'Yes . . . no, I just . . . It was close, I know it was close . . .'

Major Hunter had joined them. Pitch black, no moon – shades still in place. 'You sure about that?' he asked, his voice dry, doubtful.

'Yes!'

'You hit it?'

'I don't know!'

'You saw it, it being pitch black out there?'

'Yes! No! I don't know! It was close! I could . . . smell it. Feel it.' He looked around the little group. 'I swear to God there was something . . .'

Major Hunter took the rifle off him. He reached into one of the many pockets on his safari jacket and removed a handful of bullets. He loaded them one by one, not looking at the weapon as he did, but allowing his reflective eyes to bore into Jake.

Then he said, 'Do you want to go to your tent, Jake, let someone else take your shift? Or are you man enough to return to duty?'

Jake swallowed. 'I'm man enough,' he said, but without conviction. 'I . . . just had no bullets left . . .'

'You have now.' Major Hunter thrust the rifle into Jake's chest. 'Word of advice though. If you shoot at everything that moves, we're gonna run out of ammo pretty soon. And I'm telling you now, once we're out of bullets, you *really* don't want to be stuck out here. So if you hear something, wait till you see it, and if you see it, wait till you see the whites of its eyes before you pull the trigger. OK?'

Jake nodded.

'*OK*?'

'Yes, Major.'

Major Hunter nodded once and stalked off. Jake bit down on his lower lip and looked back out into the darkness. The others were still looking at him.

'There *was* something out there,' he said.

They all nodded. Except for Pete Windsor. He just said, 'Plonker,' before heading for his tent.

Michael knew exactly how scary it was standing guard. Katya too. They exchanged glances as Pete entered his tent. Michael didn't care if he was a Prince. All he knew was that he had an overwhelming urge to thump him.

Twice, preferably.

Chapter Eight

There was no warning shout or cry or scream. Sam, on her first tour of night duty, was either scared witless – or dead already.

Michael, unable to sleep, was tossing and turning in his tent. He was probably aware of the sound before most of the others – a distant rumble, yet so low and constant that he quickly became used to it, as if it was just another part of the aural nightscape of the jungle. Even as it grew louder and he became aware of the slight vibration through the hard ground beneath his bed roll, he was not unduly concerned.

He had experienced such movements thousands of miles away on Mount Taron just a few days before, and the instability of the earth was no longer a surprise or a cause of concern to him. Katya had already told him that the Great Rift Valley ran through Zambeziland, and minor earthquakes were to be expected.

Michael sat up. The sound was now much louder, the vibrations beneath him more pronounced and somehow more chaotic. He could hear a kind of snapping, an almost mechanical churning and stamping, as if a thousand pneumatic drills were tearing into the earth and getting closer every second.

It was not a *good* sound. It was the sound of approaching danger. Michael rolled out of his sleeping bag, pulled on his boots and top, and was just reaching for the zipped tent flaps when they magically opened and Major Hunter's head, his shades still in place, poked through.

'Get out . . . now!'

'What—?'

'*MOVE IT!*'

He withdrew, and a moment later Michael stumbled out after him. The others were appearing too – Jake, Pete, Ash, Petra and Katya, all equally disorientated. The noise was cacophonous now, and seemed to be coming from every direction.

'THIS WAY!' Major Hunter yelled, and charged towards the rear of the camp.

They went after him.

'What the hell . . . ?' Michael yelled at Katya as they fell in together.

'Elephants!' Katya shouted. 'Stampede!'

'RUN!' Major Hunter roared.

And they ran, full pelt, charging through the saw grass towards the trees, aware with every step that something massive was descending on them, some invisible force that would pound them into the ground, stamp them out of existence.

Major Hunter was the first to the small clump of trees thirty metres beyond the latrines. And the first to clamber up into them. No waiting for his charges, no making sure they were OK. He hauled himself up to safety and only then turned and bellowed at them: 'Climb! Climb!'

The ground was literally shaking now. The trees themselves were vibrating like massive tuning forks. They scrambled as best they could into the lower branches, dividing themselves between the three largest trees. Only Ash couldn't quite haul himself up, his weight and the sweat dripping from his hands made it hard for him to get a grip, and even in the dark they could see his eyes wide with panic and fright.

'I can't . . . I can't . . . !'

Katya swivelled towards Major Hunter. 'Ash! He can't make it!'

'If he wants to,' Major Hunter yelled, 'he'll do it!'

Katya looked astonished. 'You have to help him!'

The Major's sunglasses were in place, and he was absolutely unreadable. But it was clear he wasn't going to move one single centimetre to help Ash. Katya slipped down from her position of comparative safety to the lower, flimsier branches and reached down to take his hand. But he was heavy, and his hand, greasy with sweat, kept slipping from her own.

'Please!' he cried. 'Just pull me . . .'

'I'm trying!'

A bush, just a few metres away, was suddenly flattened. A huge dark hulk of a beast flashed past. Ash let out a yell and made another attempt, but he still couldn't quite get there.

A moment later Michael dropped down beside him. A fraction of a second later Jake landed beside him. Together they pushed and heaved Ash upwards, with Katya pulling from the other end, and finally, finally, he got a proper grip of her hand and managed to place his foot on a knot in the bark and was hauled up to safety. Michael and Jake clambered up after him, and not a moment too soon, as half a dozen bull elephants thundered past *exactly* where they'd been. One crashed into the trunk of the tree, almost throwing them to the ground and what would have been certain death.

Ash, between desperate gulping breaths, shouted, 'Thank you, thank you, thank you!'

The great bulk of the herd was now swirling around beneath them, battering their refuge repeatedly. Thousands of tonnes of muscle and brute force smashed everything in its path. It was all the more terrifying because they could see virtually nothing, just vague, menacing outlines in the darkness; but they could smell them and feel them and could have reached out to touch them.

'Sam!' shouted Katya. 'Where's Sam?'

'She was standing guard!' Michael yelled back. He stared out into the dense, heaving morass below. Here, perched in thick, sturdy trees, they were actually swaying with the violence of the herd's passing, as if they were clinging to plastic straws in a hurricane. If Sam was out there, if she hadn't managed to climb to safety, then she was dead, she had to be.

Then Major Hunter had the bright idea of switching on his flashlight and aiming its powerful beam across the herd – and every one of them wished he hadn't. Michael had thought there were perhaps a few dozen elephants and they had just been unfortunate to get caught up in their flight, but there were *hundreds*, perhaps even a *thousand*. A huge sea of heaving grey flesh rampaging out of control. It was much, *much* worse than he could have imagined.

Sam was not only dead. She was dead and *flat*.

And suddenly, it was over. The herd, so massive, so loud, so ground-shudderingly frightening, was gone, leaving only their stench and great, choking clouds of dust in their wake. Michael, Katya, Ash, Pete, Jake and Petra stayed exactly where they were, breathing hard despite not having exerted themselves, just gasping through the dust, exhilarated to be alive, surprised and shocked by what they had just gone through.

Petra made the first move to get down – but was stopped by an angry bellow from higher up in the trees.

'Stay where you are!' Major Hunter was barely visible against the night sky. 'We don't know what spooked them. And in case you hadn't noticed, your friend with all the piercings has our only rifle.'

Katya could see the sense in it – but it still didn't feel right. 'She's . . . out there . . .'

'We wait for daylight.'

There was to be no discussion.

Chapter Nine

It was Pete Windsor who found the rifle, nestling in the lower branches of a tree about a hundred metres out on the south western side of the camp. He let out a triumphant whoop and they all hurried over, with Major Hunter bringing up the rear. He bellowed at Pete not to touch anything. The Major, taller than all of them, reached up and carefully lifted the weapon down. He checked it, nodded, before looking further up the tree. They had spent the past two hours searching the grounds around the remains of their camp for signs of the young goth, dreading that at any moment they might stumble across her hideously trampled body. But there had been nothing until this.

'Pretty clear what happened here,' said the Major. 'She sought refuge in this baobab – when she should have been alerting us. Damn lucky I was awake and was able to save your miserable souls. But she hid up there, branch snapped – you can see where it broke – and she fell into the stampede, rifle lodged itself here on the way down. Body's been carried along with them, vultures will have it by now.' He shook his head. 'Nothing more we can do. Let's see what we can rescue from the camp.'

Katya's eyes flitted towards Michael; he tried to read what she was thinking beyond the basic anger which came with Major Hunter's dismissal of Sam's chances of survival, but couldn't quite work her out, or why she was saying nothing. It was most unlike her. Instead it was pale and sunburned Petra who spoke.

'We cannot . . . just . . . give up on her.'

Major Hunter seemed to grow a couple of extra inches. 'We do as I say.'

'Then we have to tell someone, the authorities, her parents . . . someone!'

'The authorities are three days' march from here, and we have no other means of contacting them. Her death is unfortunate, and it will be fully investigated on our return.'

'So we're going home?' Jake asked.

'No.' He let it sit like that for just long enough to be sure that any hope they had of a swift return to civilization was fully quashed. Then he nodded into the far distance. 'We're here to complete our mission. We trek. We climb Mount Zambella.' Major Hunter's voice was dry, emotionless. 'This journey we're on, it's about showing you what life is really like, and what you can learn from it. Well, we've lost someone now, and that's a harsh lesson, but it shows you how dangerous it is out here and why you have to be alert at all times. Why you have to be able to rely on your team to get you through. If Sam had been a team player, she wouldn't have hidden in a tree instead of alerting us to the stampede. She's gone now, we learn from it and we move on. Nothing to be gained by running back to base crying, you hear?'

He nodded around them all. Petra nodded, Jake and Ash too. Pete just looked at him. Katya stared at the ground. Michael grunted, and was the first to turn towards the camp. It wasn't that he was keen to carry out the Major's orders, he just needed space to think. He knew there was a *lot* about him that didn't add up. He had *wrestled* with a lion. He was a secret drinker. The elephant stampede had been beyond his control, but the way he had been the first to climb to safety, refusing to help Ash, staying up in the tree for ever when Sam was missing . . . revealed more about him than Michael almost dared contemplate. Was Major Hunter a coward? Was the bullying and the relentless discipline just a way of covering that up? The problem was that Michael could argue it both ways – by letting them sort themselves out, by alienating them, the Major might actually be making them work as a team. But was it deliberate? How was he supposed to tell? And what if something else happened?

'Michael?' He turned. Katya was beside him, the torn remnants of a tent in her hands. 'Whatever you're thinking, just remember, we're here to protect the Prince. And Major Hunter is still in charge.'

'Yes he is. Unless we disarm him and tie him up.' He looked at her. He was joking, but was interested in her reaction. She just looked at him, unreadable. He lowered his voice. 'OK, I *know* we can't do that. It's just . . . we've survived the Arctic and the rainforest – just about. But it's different out here. If we go it alone and mess it up, it won't just be the two of us that die, it'll be his Highness and the rest of them. We'd never live that down, although technically we'd probably be dead as well.' He sighed. 'OK, I guess we go with the flow for now, give him the benefit of the doubt.'

Katya was nodding, while at the same time watching the Major, who was barking out yet more orders, this time at Jake, on the far side of the camp. Nodding, but saying nothing.

'I know that look,' said Michael, 'you're having a big thought.'

'It's just stupid.'

'Well, you're the expert. *Tell.*'

She gave a little shrug. 'You think I know too much about too many different subjects. Facts.'

'Stuff.'

'Stuff. You ever heard of the tree of life?'

'Nope.'

'It's this amazing tree you find in the savannah. Huge, twenty metres tall. It looks like it has been picked out of the ground and stuffed back in upside-down.'

'Uhuh.'

'Listen to me. It's so big it can provide shelter, food and water for animals and humans alike. The bark is fire resistant, it can be made into cloth and rope. The leaves can be turned into medicine. Its fruit is known as monkey bread, rich in vitamin C. The trunk can store hundreds of litres of water you can tap into in dry periods. It's actually hollow, you can *live* in it, Michael.'

'OK, I'm impressed, Katya. What's your *point*?'

'It's proper, Latin name is *Adansonia digitata*, but it's commonly known as the baobab.'

'The . . .'

Katya was looking back towards the tree where Pete had discovered Sam's rifle. It was tall and thin with many lower branches. No fruit, no obvious water-storage capacity or inner hollowness to provide shelter.

'That's not a baobab,' said Michael.

'No.'

'He called it a baobab.'

'Exactly.'

'Worrying,' said Michael.

'I'm beginning to think,' said Katya, 'that Major Hunter hasn't a clue what he's talking about.'

Michael nodded. 'Or,' he said, 'he's testing us.'

They stared at the tree. They stared at the Major.

Michael took a deep breath. 'I'm not very good with *stuff*. But I do know about the Mutiny on the Bounty. I presume . . .'

'Captain Bligh. He was a vicious ship captain and his crew rebelled against him. Is that what you're suggesting.'

'I'm not suggesting. Just reminding you.'

'You do know how it ended for the mutineers?'

'Ahm . . .'

'They landed on a small island, a tropical paradise. And they very quickly murdered each other.'

Michael looked thoughtful. 'Well, we wouldn't murder each other. Just Pete.'

Major Hunter had his rifle slung over his shoulder, his shades in place. He looked confident, in control, ready for action. His charges, on the other hand, looked edgy, tired and scared. Until the elephant stampede, until Sam's disappearance or probable death, what they had been experiencing was little more than a camping trip. It was tough going, exhausting, but in its own way exhilarating. They had, slowly, been learning how to work together. But now . . . now there was a shadow hanging over them, a genuine fear of what lay ahead . . . and behind . . . and all around them. They weren't in a petting zoo. They couldn't phone their parents. There was nobody to turn to but themselves. They had a limited amount of food, they had little water. They had lost three tents. Their various pots and pans were scattered over a wide area, but were mostly tracked down and beaten back into shape. They had one rifle and one leader who they were beginning to have severe doubts about, a leader who was intent on leading them relentlessly further and further into the bush, away from civilisation, away from help or rescue.

They set out. Hunter forged ahead. Jake was behind him as usual, but the others now walked in pairs instead of paced out. The heat seemed more oppressive, the savannah more intimidating; they sweated, and they worried about how much they were sweating, and sweated some more. They were soaked through. They had been told to keep their fluid levels up, but water was in short supply. Twice they stopped to fill their bottles at streams.

Ash said, 'Major, should we be drinking this water? With all the bugs and stuff?'

'The locals have been drinking here for ten thousand years,' said the Major Hunter, 'they're still around, aren't they?'

'Some of them,' Pete muttered.

'What was that?' the Major snapped.

'Nothing,' said Pete. He bent to fill his bottle. The others followed suit.

The Major shook his head. 'If you have something to say, and you say it, stand by it. Don't chicken out.' He pulled his rucksack down and unzipped one of the side pockets. He pulled out a small packet and removed several tablets. 'I'm not stupid. I know your soft, middle-class bellies can't handle a little *upset*. Here.' He tossed a tablet to Pete, and then one each for the others. 'That'll kill whatever you're frightened of in the water. Cholera, typhoid, dysentery, take your pick. Unless you want to tough it out.' He looked at each one of them. Nobody was prepared to drink directly from the stream. 'Thought not. Give 'em thirty minutes to work, the water will be fine.'

He shook his head and marched on. They watched him, seething, and then followed.

'That mutiny on the Bounty?' Katya said quietly to Michael. 'I think it's getting closer.'

Chapter Ten

It was late afternoon when they heard the panicked trumpet of the elephant calf. Major Hunter waved them into a crouching position while he scuttled into a clump of bushes. After several long moments, he waved them forward and they quickly bustled up beside him, curious but also wary. Elephants had already almost killed them once and they had no particular desire to repeat the experience.

But this was different. Michael was looking down a short incline leading to a waterhole around which the vegetation in every direction had been trampled down. The herd that had passed through their camp the night before had clearly come this way, stopped briefly to drink and moved on. But the sheer weight of their numbers had churned up the ground in general and the water hole in particular, so that it was now thick with mud. A baby elephant, big as a cow but also tiny compared to the females crowding around it, had become stuck and its attempts to free itself were only making matters worse. It was squealing and crying and three females were tramping around trying to help, but without success. They were distressed not only because of its predicament, but because the rest of the herd had already moved on.

'What do we do?' Jake whispered.

'We wait and we watch,' said Major Hunter.

'We have to help,' said Katya.

'We do as I say.'

'Because it's the law of the jungle, innit?' said Pete.

Michael almost smiled. He didn't think anyone could say that with a straight face, but Pete Windsor's had never been straighter. Deep down he knew Pete was right, but it would be hard to watch a helpless creature exhaust itself and eventually die.

'If we're not going to help,' said Michael, 'then we should move on.'

Major Hunter's sunglasses turned towards him.

'We moved on from Sam pretty quick too,' said Katya, her voice small but laced with accusation.

Major Hunter's sunglasses moved to her. His mouth

visibly tightened. 'You know much about elephants, Katya?'

'Some.'

'You know about allomothers?'

Katya swallowed. 'No.'

'The calf is an orphan, otherwise it would only be the mother trying to help. These three are allomothers, they take responsibility for the calf if something happens to the real mother. Elephants are born with fewer survival instincts than most animals, they need help. They're trying to work out what to do, we need to see what they come up with.'

'Teamwork,' said Jake.

Under his breath Pete said, 'Teacher's pet.'

Under *his* breath Ash said, 'Why does everything have to be a lesson?'

The calf squealed again. The allomothers stepped warily around their charge. The waterhole was small enough for them to get around behind the calf and push it, but the mud was so thick and turgid and had risen so far up its young body that it was impossible to dislodge.

They worked, and they paced, and they trumpeted, and they worked some more, but it was impossible.

Major Hunter and the trekkers lay in the bushes,

grateful for the rest and grimly fascinated by the elephants' efforts and the calf's slow decline.

Katya could not resist giving a running commentary, and for once Major Hunter said nothing, seemingly content to listen and watch.

'The trunk,' Katya said, 'is like a fusion of the nose and upper lip, they use it for everything – sensitive enough to pick up a single blade of grass, yet strong enough to rip the branches off a tree. They use it to tear up their food and place it in their mouth. If the food is, like, too high up a tree, it'll wrap it's trunk around the tree and shake it until it comes loose. Or the entire tree comes down.'

'Powerful,' said Petra. 'Smart.'

'Not smart enough to get the baby out of the mud,' said Pete. 'No opposable thumbs, see?' He held up his hands. 'Otherwise they'd make themselves some spades and dig him out.'

They all gave him a look.

They watched, and they waited.

The struggles of the baby elephant grew weaker, and weaker, until finally it lay completely motionless. If anything, it had sunk deeper into the waterhole, and the mud was now up around its neck. As the day had gone on, the mud had thickened in the heat, pressing on the creature's chest and making it difficult to breathe. Now it only occasionally let out dry gasps. Its small trunk lay flaccidly atop the corrugating mud, its emaciated ears flat out, only occasionally twitching. The allomothers had stayed loyally by its side all day, but now they too were sensing that their fight was unwinnable, that death was approaching and that they would have to leave or get left behind by the herd.

One by one, they approached the calf, and patted it with their trunks. It made a feeble effort to return their affections. Michael, glancing at Katya, saw that she had tears in her eyes. Nobody spoke as the allomothers drifted sombrely into the encroaching darkness.

Their group remained silently watching for several minutes.

It was Katya who finally spoke. 'Can't we do some—?'

'*Shhhhh!*' Major Hunter had his finger to his lips. Katya was about to hiss something back at him, but he nodded forward, and they all looked where they thought he was looking, their eyes straining for some hopeful movement from the elephant, but it was still lying deathly still. Then Michael spotted something even further away, emerging from a tangle of bushes and moving low through the trampled grass – the unmistakable outline of a big cat. Michael nudged Katya and pointed.

'Lion,' he whispered, needlessly.

'Everyone just keep quiet and calm,' said Major Hunter. He had slipped his rifle off his shoulder and raised it.

'Maybe it's just coming to drink,' said Katya.

Major Hunter shook his head. 'Defenceless animal, brink of death, a lion can smell it a mile away. While we've been watching, she's been watching too, just waiting for the allomothers to leave.'

He set himself comfortably on the ground and raised the rifle back to his shoulder and focussed in.

'What . . . what're you going to do?' Ash asked.

Major Hunter's sunglasses moved towards him. 'What do *you* think I should do?'

Ash's eyes darted from the lion to the Major to the helpless calf and back. 'I don't—'

'Kill the calf? Put it out of it's misery?'

'No, I—'

'Kill the lion? King of the jungle, getting rarer every day, kill it for doing what it does naturally? It's the circle of life, *boy*. Or do nothing? Maybe I shouldn't be wasting one of our precious bullets? Maybe we're going to need it, eh? Tell you what – you decide.'

Ash was breathing hard. The lion was almost upon the elephant, which had rallied enough to begin squealing.

'Warning shot!' Ash suddenly exclaimed.

'Waste a bullet?' said Major Hunter.

'Put it out of its misery,' said Pete Windsor.

'Best thing,' said Jake, 'it's nearly dead anyway.'

The lion was circling in, focussed on its helpless prey, but also constantly aware of its surroundings. It might have been the king of the jungle, but a wise king chooses his battles well. The lion knew it wasn't a match for a rampaging elephant, so it was constantly on the verge of fight or flight. It was all about survival.

Major Hunter focussed his sights on the calf. Michael noticed a bead of sweat running down the side of his face. Abruptly he dropped the rifle from his shoulder and held it out to the young Royal.

'Here, Pete,' he said, 'you take the shot.'

'Me? But I've never—'

'Take it. One shot. Make it count.'

Pete took the rifle, held it momentarily against his chest, then quickly snapped it into position. His eye moved to the sight, his finger to the trigger. The calf, which they'd thought to be on the verge of death, suddenly spotted the approaching lion and began squealing and slapping its trunk uselessly against the thick mud.

'Do it,' said Jake.

Pete began to squeeze the trigger.

Michael knew exactly what Major Hunter was doing, and he hated him for it. He was determined to make them stronger people, he was teaching them about bravery and survival. It was a lesson in life. But Michael was sick to death of his lessons, fed up with him trying to turn every experience into a team-building exercise.

'Pete! Take the shot!' hissed Katya.

The lion was right up beside the baby now, ready to tear into it.

'Shoot!' cried Ash. 'I've seen what they do on TV, it's horrible, Pete, please just . . .'

Pete lowered the rifle. He shook his head. 'I can't,' he said quietly. 'I can't kill a baby elephant. I can't . . .' He looked directly at Major Hunter. 'And you don't want me to. Because it's . . . it's the circle of life, isn't it? It's how it has to be.'

Major Hunter nodded. Another lesson. Michael hated him even more. The anger boiled up in him, and without even properly thinking about it he grabbed the rifle out of Pete's hands.

'Don't you—' Major Hunter spat, but before he could finish Michael had snapped the rifle to his shoulder, aimed and pulled the trigger. The bullet exploded out of the chamber, the rifle kicked back, and less than a hundred metres away the lion visibly jumped, before bolting away into the bushes.

The others were looking at him in shock.

'Did you hit it?' Katya asked.

Michael said nothing.

Major Hunter ripped the rifle out of Michael's hands. His lip curled up in disgust. 'He missed. He wasted a bullet and he missed.'

'No, I didn't,' said Michael.

'You panicked and didn't take aim properly.'

'No,' said Michael. 'I missed deliberately. I scared off the lion. I used one bullet and saved two lives.'

Major Hunter's eyes were, as ever, hidden behind his sunglasses. Was he about to lash out at Michael's rebellion and nerve or let it ride and exact his revenge later, when there were no witnesses? But when he spoke, his words were completely unexpected.

'Very good, Michael. You read the situation well, you used the bullet effectively, there was no need to kill. Now what?'

'Now . . . what do you mean?'

'How do you follow up?'

'The elephant . . . ? Try and save it . . . ?'

'And how do we do that?' He nodded around the small group.

'Teamwork?' ventured Ash.

Major Hunter nodded again. 'But first?'

'We set up a perimeter,' said Jake, 'make sure the lion doesn't come back.'

Michael looked at Katya. She had a bemused expression on her face. He knew she was thinking the same thing about the Major – that he had just handed them another life lesson.

'OK then, you're on your own, let's see what you can do.'

Michael held on to the rifle as they hurried forward and gathered around the trapped elephant. It was now too exhausted to even register their presence. Almost instinctively the girls knelt beside it and petted and patted it before quite self consciously realizing that it wasn't helping, and getting back to their feet. Katya especially was full of ideas. She realized the importance of keeping the calf hydrated, and sent Ash to the other side of the waterhole to collect water, using one of the saucepans that had survived the stampede. She dispatched Petra and Jake towards some nearby trees to collect vines and strong, sinewy branches to use as ropes, although only after Michael had scoped out the area for signs of the lion. They had one collapsible shovel between them, so had to fashion digging implements out of large, flat stones.

They dug. They pulled. They poured cool water over the elephant. They dug. They pulled. They sweated. They dug. They pulled. They sweated.

Michael looked at Katya and said, 'If Major Hunter was stuck in the mud, I'm not sure we'd make this much effort.'

From a hundred metres away Major Hunter said, 'I'm not deaf.'

Michael put some extra effort into the digging. Katya snorted.

They worked themselves to exhaustion even as the sun baked the mud harder, squeezing the elephant's barely grown lungs with ever greater pressure. Its breathing, already laboured, grew increasingly shallow.

Every five minutes Michael stopped digging to patrol the perimeter. After a while, Ash, his arms aching, asked if he could take over the guard duty. Michael responded by nodding ahead of him. Ash followed his gaze. At first he could see nothing, but then, as Michael pointed, he picked out a very slight movement in the undergrowth about two hundred metres away. The lion, waiting patiently. But Michael wasn't finished – he nodded in exactly the opposite direction and then there was no mistaking what Ash was seeing. One of the allomothers, massive and grey and wrinkled, was waiting in the shade of some trees, watching.

'If they both attack at once,' said Michael, 'you think you can handle it?'

Ash looked back to the lion, and then returned his gaze to the elephant. 'I think,' he said quietly, 'that you're probably the better shot.' He gave a short nod and returned to the digging with renewed vigour.

Michael kept his eyes roving between the two mighty beasts and the rescue effort – and occasionally allowed them to flick towards Major Hunter, now in his usual place – perched in a tree, either keeping his own watchful eye or drinking again. At the water hole, Katya was covered from head to foot in thick, glutinous mud. She paused for just a moment to remove a red bandana from around her neck and wipe it across her brow. She smiled across at him. She was, he thought, much more of a natural leader than he was: she was efficient, organized and inspiring.

He didn't smile back. He didn't want to give her too much encouragement.

'Look at his eyes,' said Petra, 'they're begging us to hurry.'

'He's a she,' said Katya.

'How can you tell?'

'Takes one to know one,' said Pete.

If any of the others had said it, they might well have laughed. But coming from Pete Windsor, it fell completely flat. Nobody seemed to like him very much. He was, literally, a royal pain in the ass.

And then there was shouting and clapping and Katya was screaming, 'Don't stop! Don't stop!'

Michael charged across from the perimeter to help with the final effort to haul the swollen and exhausted baby elephant free of the hellish suction and compression of mud. With one massive, final effort the calf finally just shot out the last few feet, as if the waterhole was admitting defeat. She stood shakily at the centre of the little group, and then collapsed back to her knees utterly exhausted.

'Don't let her lie down!' Katya urged. 'Get her up!'

They pulled her back up and held her there while the blood surged back into her numb legs. Petra began to pour water over her from the saucepan, and then they all laughed as the baby's trunk, until then hanging flaccidly, suddenly reached up and plunged into it and began to suck greedily.

Katya had tears on her cheeks. She reached down and kissed the top of the elephant's head. Then she removed her red bandana and tied it around one of the small protuberances which would one day grow into tusks. 'Your name is . . .' Katya looked up at her comrades.

'Tusker,' said Ash.

The others nodded their approval. 'Tusker,' said Katya. 'May you live long and prosper.'

Pete said, 'Is that from *Star Wars*?'

'*Star Trek*,' said Petra.

Major Hunter called across from his perch. 'She's not a pet! Let her go! And if you lot had been paying attention, you'd know we got company.'

Michael's stomach turned over. In the excitement of freeing Tusker, he'd neglected his duty. He turned to find that the allomother had, very, very quietly, moved within just a few dozen metres of the waterhole and was now doing a weird kind of a dance, moving from one massive foot to the other. It was difficult to tell if she was showing excitement at the survival of the calf or was preparing to attack.

Michael slowly raised the rifle – but then immediately felt a hand on his shoulder.

'No,' said Katya. She patted the calf firmly on the rump. Tusker gave a surprised little jump before quickly trotting forward to shelter between the enormous legs of her adopted mother. The huge creature and its new charge, decorated with the small red bandana, stood looking back at the mud splattered teenagers for a long moment. Then the allomother raised its trunk and let out a tremendous blast of sound that shook them all, before turning to begin a leisurely pursuit of their herd.

Chapter Eleven

'It's not a crisis until we know something for definite,' said Bonsoir.

'You really believe that?' asked Bailey.

Bonsoir hesitated before shaking his head. 'No. You're right. It's definitely a crisis.'

They had just emerged from a meeting with Dr Kincaid and the other Artists, called to discuss the curious case of Major Hunter, and how there appeared to be two of him. One was a larger than life, quick to anger, internationally renowned hunter, tracker and survival expert, and the other, either by accident or design, was an imposter. One had been given security clearance eight weeks earlier by the British Secret Service. The other hadn't.

Major Hunter – that is, the real one, the one who could track wild animals and was at home in the wilderness – was as helpful as he could be, but nothing he said gave them much encouragement. He painstakingly explained for the third time how he had sold his business to a man he had never met, a man called Alger Hess. The transaction had been carried out initially by e-mail, and then papers had been transferred via lawyers while the real Major Hunter was on what he thought then was his final trek across the savannah.

'How did you come into contact with him in the first place?' Dr Kincaid asked.

'Through my website. Guess he caught me at the right time – I was just back from a trek, I was exhausted. I've been doing this for twenty-five years, and I had just gotten to the point where I fancied having a bath where there wasn't a good chance of having to fight off a hippo while I was having it. And besides, the offer he made was for enough for me to be able to retire in considerable style. So I snapped it up.'

'You didn't check him out?'

'Far as I could. He said he worked in the same field, but in a different part of Africa, a country he had to get out of because a civil war broke out. It sounded pretty dangerous. He had references from past clients. He said he'd worked with kids before, had a real interest in sorting them out. He sounded perfect. '

'Those kids,' said Dr Kincaid, 'their parents hired Major Hunter, not Alger Hess.'

'And they got Major Hunter. When he bought the company, he got the rights to the name. Dr Kincaid, you're a businessman, you know how it works. You don't expect to meet Ronald McDonald every time you go into McDonalds.'

Dr Kincaid let out a sigh. 'Except we're not talking about burgers. We're talking about kids. Kids in danger because you didn't run a proper background check. In danger because you preferred to take the money and run.'

Their eyes met and locked.

'I don't run anywhere,' Major Hunter growled. And then a moment later added, 'Unless I'm being chased by a lion.' He smiled suddenly and unexpectedly. 'Hey,' he said, 'I made a mistake. No use dwelling on it. I have a problem, I don't cry about it. I sort it out. They're out there somewhere. OK, they're at the mercy of everything Mother Nature has to throw at them, and they're being guided by the mysterious Alger Hess. He might just be as great a survival expert as I am, but might equally be a madman or a spy or an international terrorist who wouldn't know an ostrich from a baboon.' He looked at each one of the Artists, finishing up on

Dr Kincaid. 'It's a mess all right. Anything else I need to know?'

'One of the boys is a member of the British Royal Family.'

'Excellent!' Major Hunter clapped his hands together. 'That means there might be a reward! I knew I retired too soon!'

Chapter Twelve

Mount Zambella began to fill so much of their forward vision that they were half fooled into thinking that it might only be a few hours' march away. But if Major Hunter knew exactly how far they had yet to go he didn't say, and they were too afraid of a savage put down to ask. All they knew was that they had to climb it, and not one of them was looking forward to it. They had already experienced too much, and they knew instinctively that things could only get worse.

They camped that night in a dried-up riverbed, clearing away rocks and boulders to pitch their tents in the dust. The thinking was that with bullets in short supply, they needed as much open space around them as possible so that they could detect approaching danger. In this they were also aided by a full moon. They built a large campfire and ate from their dwindling rations.

'Tomorrow,' said Major Hunter, 'we hunt. And by *we* I mean *you*. You track, you set traps and if you're absolutely confident of your ability to shoot a living creature on the move, you use the rifle. But remember, we only have six bullets left. The more you use, the closer we come to being the hunted, not the hunters.'

That didn't help their mood. Major Hunter grunted and went off to his tent. It was only when they heard the steady rhythm of his snores twenty minutes later that they began to open up again. Surprisingly, considering how close he had kept to the Major, it was Jake who spoke.

'Hardly any food, water, bullets, and all the time heading away from what passes for civilisation around here.' He shook his head. 'I don't like it.'

'Food, water, bullets . . . and one of us dead.'

'Missing,' said Michael.

'Trampled,' said Petra. 'Dead.'

'We're not on a trek any more,' said Ash, 'we're like prisoners on a death march.'

'Death march!' Pete Windsor snorted. 'Have we been eaten? Are we actually starving or dehydrated?'

'Well, I don't know about you,' Ash began, 'but I could eat a—'

'Listen to me,' Pete growled. 'None of you are seeing

the bigger picture. This is all one big game. This is the twenty-first century, they're not just going to let us wander around out here without some kind of back-up plan. I don't think Sam is dead. Maybe she was injured and she's been airlifted out. Or more likely, she's a plant, put here to scare the life out of us by disappearing. It's another one of his lessons. She's in a hotel somewhere, living it up. When we get home she'll pop up laughing at what suckers we were. And who says we've only got six bullets left? The Major's just trying to frighten us. He wants us to man-up, that's all. Man-up.'

To date Pete had behaved like a loud-mouthed idiot and everyone hated him. Now for the first time he was contributing something other than verbal abuse. For nearly a minute nobody responded: everyone was thinking it through.

Then Ash spoke. 'He couldn't have planned the elephant stampede. *Could* he?'

'I think he's capable of anything,' said Petra.

'Maybe he just took advantage of it to allow Sam to slip away,' said Jake.

They exchanged glances. It was too incredible to be true. Surely.

'OK,' said Katya. '*If* this is all a set-up, then we have

to prove it. Find his extra ammo. His satellite phone. His GPS.'

They all nodded. Except Michael.

'Alternatively,' he said, 'perhaps *this* is his plan. He wants us to bond, then work together as a team to expose him.'

Katya stood up. 'Either way,' she said with finality. 'We need to know.'

Major Hunter had to be separated from his rucksack. If he had spare bullets, or a mobile phone, that's where they had to be. They had to lure him away from it. They would have to watch and wait for their opportunity. Then it would be down to good luck, with a little bravery thrown in. They all turned to look at his tent. He was still snoring loudly. They agreed to wait for daylight.

Someone was shaking him in the dark.

Then Ash's voice, a mildly panicked whisper. 'Michael . . . Wake-up . . . Michael . . .'

Ash's flashlight came on, blinding him. Michael sat up and pushed the torch out of his face. He shook himself. He wasn't sure how long he'd been asleep. His first thought was that Ash must have foolishly gone and tried to search Major Hunter's rucksack himself and was now terrified because he'd been spotted. But then he realized that Ash was soaked to the skin and outside he could hear the thunderous sound of torrential rain. It was coming back to him now. Ash had been on guard duty. It was Michael's turn to take over.

'It's OK, I'll be there in a minute.'

'Michael! You have to come. The river . . . the river bed is starting to fill . . .'

Michael sat up. He began to pull on his trousers and boots. 'What does Major Hunter say?'

'I haven't asked him.'

'Ash! He's still in charge . . .'

'I just didn't want to be shouted at, you know what he's like, and it might be nothing.'

Michael climbed out of the tent.

It wasn't *nothing*.

The moment he stepped onto what had been the dried-out river bed, the water seeped up over his boots and mud sucked at them as he strode forward. The rain cascaded down, instantly soaking the rest of him. The moon was hidden by black storm clouds. He took Ash's flashlight and shone it in every direction.

Not good.

Not good *at all*.

He sensed movement behind him and turned to find Katya hurrying up. 'What are you thinking?' she asked.

'I'm thinking we either find a boat or get the hell out of here.'

'Do you want to tell the Major, or let him float away?'

'Don't tempt me. I'll tell him. You wake the others. And hurry.'

'Yes, sir,' she said.

Michael smiled after her before hurrying to the Major's tent. He unzipped the front and leaned in. Immediately he was assailed by stale alcohol fumes and the foghorn blast of snoring. Michael's flashlight centred on the Major's face: he couldn't believe he was *still* wearing his sunglasses. He moved the light around the tent: it settled on his rucksack. Now might be the perfect time to . . .

As if even thinking it was a crime, the Major suddenly reared up. 'What . . . what?!' he cried, his hand already snaking out for the rifle he hoped to find by his side, but which Ash had been using on guard duty.

'Major, it's OK . . . it's me, Michael.' He shone the torch on his own face. 'Heavy rain outside. We may have a bit of a flood problem. We need to move to higher ground.'

Michael moved the torch back to the Major. His face was suddenly suffused with anger.

'Why didn't that god-damn chicken wake me himself?'

'He tried to,' Michael lied, 'but you were too drunk.'

It was out before he could stop himself. His own mouth dropped open in surprise. There were about five seconds where the Major didn't react at all . . . and then suddenly Michael was lying on his back in three inches of water and mud outside the tent, dazed, confused and with his jaw aching.

Major Hunter loomed over him. 'Don't you ever . . . *ever* . . . speak to—'

The Major stopped abruptly. His eyes flitted up. And widened. Michael's head swivelled back, the pain forgotten.

Thundering towards them, as if someone had smashed a dam: a huge, solid wall of water.

Above the cacophony of sound, Katya's voice: 'Flash flood! Run for your lives!'

In an instant, Major Hunter was gone, racing for the bank.

Then they were all running.

And then, just as swiftly, they weren't – they

were swallowed whole by the raging torrent and swept away.

Chapter Thirteen

Michael was wracked by heaving spasms. He was groggy from the effort of fighting the current, sore from the pummelling he had received from the rocks and boulders and debris caught up in the flash flood. He had known even as he hurtled along that he didn't have the strength to pull himself out of the maelstrom. It was too fast; too powerful and violent. And yet here he was, alive, retching in the soft mud and dank vegetation on the riverbank; safe again, a survivor.

Once before, when he was still a reluctant pupil at boarding school, he had somehow gone beyond the normal endurance of the human body by diving repeatedly into freezing water to save the lives of fellow pupils – but he hadn't remember doing it later. He was a hero, but had acted like some kind of pre-programmed automaton. Had it happened again, only this time the only person he had saved was himself?

The answer came with the flashlight shone in his face. Someone else had saved him, and he was suddenly quite certain who it was. Of course it had to be the one man he didn't want to owe anything to – Major Hunter. He was bigger, stronger, more experienced; he was the only one of them knowledgeable enough about the way a flash flood might—

'You OK?'

No, not Major Hunter.

A girl's voice.

A *familiar* girl's voice.

Not Katya. Not Petra.

But no . . . that was *impossible* . . .

'*Sam* . . . ?'

She shone the light on her own face. 'Surprised?'

Michael forced himself to sit up. He was drenched and freezing and exhausted and confused . . . but also exhilarated. He could feel the adrenaline rushing through him. He smiled broadly.

'How are you . . . what did— the eleph— the others, are they . . . ?'

'I don't know about the others, and I only caught you by chance. I was washed along before the river got too bad and managed to drag myself out, then it really let go, and next thing I see you bobbing along. So I fished you out with the aid of a handy branch and a lot of swearing.'

Michael spat out another mouthful of river gunge before studying Samantha.

'But you're dead.'

'Not quite.'

'The stampede . . .'

'Was very useful.'

'Useful?'

'It allowed me to disappear.'

'Dis— but why would you . . . ?'

'Because I was sick of the Major ordering everyone around. I get enough of that at home.'

'But how did you survive without food or water or . . . ?'

'Easy. First of all, you're probably thinking the elephants carried off all the missing tents and supplies. Nope. I bagged a tent before you got back to the camp. Helped myself to some of the supplies too. Just my fair share.'

'So you've been following us?'

'Yep. It was easy. You make as much noise as a herd of elephants.'

'But all alone out there . . . predators . . .'

'First off, I'm used to being alone. Doesn't worry me in the slightest. And second,' she reached behind her for something sticking into the top of her trousers but covered by the back of her shirt, 'I have this . . .'

She held it up.

A revolver.

'Where the hell did you get that?!'

'Major Hunter's rucksack. While you lot were hiding in the trees I was doing a little investigating of my own. Something about him just didn't add up. So I found the gun, and I also came across this . . .'

She delved into another pocket and produced a small black, slightly mangled plastic box with a cracked screen on the front.

'GPS! I knew it!'

'Which begs the question, is it just there for back-up, or now that it's obviously broken, does he have a clue where he's taking you?'

'You? Us, surely? You're rejoining the pack?'

Sam took a deep breath. 'If there is a pack.'

Katya stood shivering, hugging herself, and staring into the fast receding waters.

Michael, Michael, Michael, Michael.
Come back. Come back now.

She refused to believe he was dead. He was too strong. He had the survival gene. And he had luck. He always had luck. She had scrambled onto the river bank just as the torrent struck and had seen him not only carried away but sucked under. Every sensible part of her knew that he had to be dead. But she still had instinct, and somehow it was booming into her heart that he was still alive, still out there, still itching to open his big mouth and cause more trouble. She glanced behind her. In the eerie, misty first-light, Jake, Petra, Ash and Pete made for a sorry looking bunch indeed. They were damp, cold and bruised. They felt very much alone. For all the bad things they'd said about Major Hunter, he was still their leader, the man who, when they got into a tight corner, exactly like this, they expected to protect them. But Major Hunter was gone too, flushed away with Michael.

They didn't know exactly where they were or what direction to walk in. Ash was on the verge of tears. Pete noticed and made a snide comment. Petra slapped his face. Pete went to slap her back but Jake caught his arm. In moments they were both rolling around in the mud punching at each other. The others shouted at them to stop, and then changed their minds and yelled at Jake to hit him harder. It was this noise that drew

Michael and Sam to them, and they stood in the bushes twenty metres away watching the fight and nudging each other, trying to decide whether to make their entry immediately or wait to see who won. They had walked for an hour upstream – and it was a stream now; the river had lost most of its strength and soon it would stop entirely, and turn to mud, and then harden. But there was still time to marvel at how the parched savannah had suddenly transformed itself. Flowers had bloomed instantly. Everything was brilliantly green and vibrant. It was almost as if they had been transported to an entirely new world.

Michael stepped into the clearing by the river. Ash noticed him first. His mouth dropped open a fraction before he pointed and yelled his name. Katya and Petra immediately turned. The fighters stopped throwing punches. A moment later Katya charged forward and threw herself at Michael. Not entirely sure if he was being attacked, Michael just stood there as she wrapped her arms around him and shrieked: 'I thought you were dead!'

And he mumbled, 'No.'

And Katya, realizing what she'd done, suddenly let go and slipped back to the ground, hurriedly adding, 'You took your time!'

Jake and Pete seemed to have forgotten their fight. They playfully punched his arms and ruffled his hair.

Katya now stood with her arms folded.

'I don't suppose you found Major Hunter on your travels?'

'Nope. But I'll tell you who I did find.'

He turned and signalled to the bushes, and Sam stepped out, smiling bashfully.

At least for a little while, being cold and damp and exhausted and hungry and thirsty didn't seem to matter quite so much.

The sun rose steadily and as the mist dissipated, the heat of the new day began to dry them out, raising their spirits still further. Katya moved into super-efficient mode, rallying them, inspiring them, directing them. For the most part they were happy that someone was taking command. Even Michael didn't mind being bossed around, because every time she asked him to do something he said he would do it in exchange for another hug and she would scowl at him, her cheeks reddening. He was *loving* it.

Katya divided them into two teams and sent them to either side of the river bank to search for Major Hunter and whatever supplies or equipment they could find.

When they re-grouped a couple of hours later, gathering round a large rock in the middle of the now dried-out river bed they had virtually nothing to show for their endeavours. No sign of the Major, two waterlogged sleeping bags and a ripped tent that was well beyond repair.

'OK,' said Katya, perching herself on the rock so that she was looking down on them, 'now we have to decide what to do next.'

'Isn't it obvious?' said Pete. 'We head back in the direction we came in.'

'Do you even know which direction we came in?' Michael asked.

Pete pointed vaguely to his left. 'Thataway?'

Ash snorted. Pete waved a warning finger at him.

'Maybe,' said Petra, 'we should stay exactly where we are – isn't that what you're supposed to do, stay put and wait to be rescued?'

'Yep,' said Katya, 'under normal circumstances. Except nobody knows we're in trouble, so they're not going to start looking for us until after we were due to return, and that's not for five days yet.'

'Well, what then?' asked Jake. 'Even if we knew what direction to walk back in, it's still going to take us three or four days, and that's without food or water, and

Major's Hunter's rifle was flushed away with him, so how are we going to protect ourselves against . . . you know . . .' He raised his hand and made a clawing motion.

'Maybe with this?' Sam cautiously raised her revolver.

'How did you get that?' Ash asked.

'Found it,' said Sam, innocently.

'Stole it,' said Michael. 'From Major Hunter's rucksack.'

'Excellent!' said Pete. 'Do you want me to carry it?'

'No,' said Sam.

'Do you even know how to use it?' Pete asked.

'Yep. Do you?'

'Of course. My neighbourhood, everyone has one, don't they?'

Michael and Katya exchanged glances. Pete was acting tough, but they both knew he was talking about the guards at Buckingham Palace.

'We take turns,' said Katya. 'And if you're not confident in your ability to use it, I'll show you how.'

The others nodded. Michael smiled to himself. Katya was doing exactly what Major Hunter had been trying to do – building confidence and team spirit, except she was doing it without bullying them or trying to make them look foolish.

Katya held her hand out for the revolver and Sam handed it over without complaint. Katya weighed it in her palm. 'It's a Smith and Wesson with a twelve bullet clip. It's not ideal for hunting, better for short range. So we'll keep it for protection, for use only as a last resort. But we still have to eat. I don't think we've the time to set traps, so we're going to have to scavenge as we walk.'

'Scavenge what?' Pete demanded. 'Are you some kind of survival expert?'

'Yes,' said Katya.

'What a load of bull,' Pete snapped.

'I could eat a load of bull,' said Ash.

And that at least raised a smile from everyone, even Pete. He blew air out of his cheeks and said: 'OK, have it your way. But if we all starve to death, I'm blaming you.'

Katya laughed. 'Fair enough,' she said. 'OK. We'd better start walking, make some ground before it gets too hot.'

'I thought we didn't know where we were?' Jake asked. 'What's the point in . . . ?'

In response Katya turned and pointed to her right. In the far distance, its snowy peak hidden by cloud, was Mount Zambella.

'We're going to climb it,' she said quietly.

'*Climb* it?' Ash asked incredulously. 'Are you out of your mind? We've no food, no water, no equipment and a poxy little gun to protect us, how are we going to climb a mountain?!'

Katya turned. 'Try and keep calm, Ash, would you? Now it's quite simple. Nobody knows where we are or what has happened to us. As far as anyone is concerned we're still trekking across the savannah and turning into better, more responsible individuals as we go. They don't expect to hear from us until we climb that mountain, just like Major Hunter told them we would. We are expected to be on top of that mountain on a certain date, and that's exactly where we are going to be – even if it kills us.'

Chapter Fourteen

Bailey really didn't like the savannah. There was no *challenge*. He liked having to land the SOS chopper in difficult locations under terrible conditions. He enjoyed hurricanes, he loved earthquakes and he was especially fond of tidal waves. Here, there was no wind, not much in the way of trees. It was flat, flat, flat; just long uninterrupted stretches of grassland. He supposed, as he brought the helicopter down in a swirl of red dust, there was at least the outside chance of being eaten by a lion.

As the chopper settled, his passengers disembarked and began to spread out. Bailey yawned. It was the eighth time that morning they'd landed like this in roughly similar surroundings, always searching for some evidence that the trekkers had passed this way. Each time they had found nothing and had to re-embark with their hearts a little heavier. The phoney Major Hunter, Alger Hess, wasn't taking his charges via the routes the real Major Hunter had established over twenty years in the survival business.

Shortly after dawn, they had broken into the offices formerly used by Major Hunter to run his business and found them deserted. His staff had been sacked and his answer machine, which was just about the only thing left in the empty offices, was jammed with messages from parents or guardians worried that they hadn't received any news at all from their children.

Major Hunter was incredulous. 'It's a basic part of the programme! You tell the kids there's no way to contact their folks, because otherwise they'll be whining to them all the time about how tough it is, but in reality you make sure the parents are kept well informed. The kids are supposed to be electronically tracked! I always meet up with my staff while the kids are sleeping and give them progress reports. This guy's either an amateur, or he knows exactly what he's doing. Which isn't good.' Major Hunter took a deep breath. He rubbed at his jaw. 'OK, at least we know the point from which they started out. They could have gone in any direction from there, except south – that would take them back to the city. There's a vast swathe of savannah between their start point and the coast on the west, and the mountains to the north. Without tracking devices, we're almost literally looking for a needle in a haystack.'

Bailey had been involved in enough rescue missions involving capsized boats on seemingly tranquil oceans to know how difficult it was to find anyone on a largely featureless canvas. You needed a distress flare, you needed a marker beacon, you needed something large and colourful to attract your attention.

'Anything?' Dr Faustus asked for the hundredth time that morning as they lifted off again and began to scan the next stretch of grassland.

'Yep,' said Bailey. 'If you're looking for a giraffe.'

Apart from Bailey, they all had binoculars clamped to their eyes. They saw rhino, zebra, gazelles, lions and elephants. It would have been breathtaking, if they hadn't been holding their breath.

'It's a paradise all right,' said Major Hunter, 'except it's one that can kill you a thousand different ways.'

'Kill *you* maybe,' said Mr Crown.

They locked eyes. For about twenty seconds. Then Mr Crown winked, and Major Hunter exploded into laughter.

Bonsoir, who'd been talking on his satellite phone,

cut the line, shook his head at the two huge men in front of him, then moved forward to speak to Dr Kincaid. The SOS founder lowered his glasses and looked hopefully at his colleague.

'Anything?'

'Plenty. But not great. Been talking to HQ. Alger Hess is even more of a mystery than we thought. He's of German extraction, but has a UK passport. Lives in Surrey, not married. Until six months ago he was an accountant in London, then suddenly resigned and dropped out of sight.'

'Until now.'

'We've been through every database we can think of, every security organization. Nothing from MI5 or MI6 or the CIA, FBI, the Russians haven't heard of him, nothing in the Middle East. We've drawn a blank.'

'Well, he's clearly not an accountant.'

'It's as if he blinked out of existence.'

Dr Kincaid sighed and looked back at the savannah racing past below. 'He's certainly done that.' He ground his fist into his leg. 'What is he? What does he want? Why hasn't he been in touch? He has a member of the Royal family, but is it a kidnapping, an assassination, blackmail, some kind of religious protest? And where's he going? There are two or three borders with unstable countries he can make for, maybe sell our Royal on to the highest bidder?' He shook his head, then looked back at Bonsoir and fixed him with a steady look. 'Did I make a mistake sending Katya and Michael alone, with no back-up?'

'No, the mistake was not checking out the Major thoroughly.' Dr Kincaid nodded grimly. 'But Katya's not stupid. She'll have worked out something isn't right. She'll deal with it.'

'And Michael?'

'If anyone knows how to put a spanner in the works, it's him.'

'Good. Then there's nothing to worry about.'

Dr Kincaid returned his attention to the window.

'There!'

It was Mr Crown who spotted a flash of red and a glint of something metallic. Nobody else could see it, and when he looked again he couldn't either. But it was a hint of something, and it was one hundred per cent more than they already had.

'Take us down, Bailey,' said Dr Kincaid.

The pilot, getting a rush of adrenaline for the first time that day, circled back, this time with Mr Crown at his shoulder, directing him down. They landed about a hundred metres from several clumps of trees which had once been surrounded by tall saw grass, but which had recently been trampled flat.

'Large herd passed this way,' said Major Hunter, 'and from the spread of their prints, the damage and the dung, I'd say it was a stampede. We're talking three or four hundred. Lets follow the tracks a bit, see where they take us.'

Dr Kincaid instructed Bailey to stay with the chopper.

'Why? Who's gonna steal it out here – monkeys?'

'They'd probably fly it better,' Mr Crown growled.

Bailey smiled after Major Hunter and his fellow Artists as they moved away from the chopper. He wanted to be with them, but his first duty was to his helicopter. He glanced up at the trees, looking for signs of monkeys.

The elephant stampede had covered such a wide expanse of ground that a blind man in a coal mine could have followed their tracks. Major Hunter ordered them to spread out. They walked twenty metres apart, marvelling at the destruction the herd had caused, but it was mixed with dread at what that might mean for the missing trekkers.

They'd been walking for ten minutes when Major Hunter held his hand up for them to stop before crouching down to scan the ground.

'Lion tracks superimposed; they're fresh. Be aware, folks. They're ambush predators, they'll be on you before you even know about it. Stand tall, don't give them an easy target.'

Bonsoir swallowed. He was brave enough, but facts and figures were his perfect world. He raised his rifle to his shoulder and began to scan the terrain ahead, then dropped it again when he saw the others weren't following suit.

A hundred metres further on, Dr Kincaid stumbled upon what Mr Crown had seen from the air. When the others hurried up they saw that he was staring at the shredded remnants of a red tent, and just to the side of it, a saucepan that had been hammered flat.

'Doesn't look good,' he said.

Major Hunter disagreed. 'Damage to property means nothing. They're out there, we have a point of reference now, they're on foot, they can't have gone that far. This is good news, people. Let's get back in the air.'

Ten minutes later it was Major Hunter himself who said, 'Bring her down, *now*.'

He could now see the dust clouds being kicked up by the herd about ten miles ahead of them, but it was something else that caught his attention.

'What is it?' Dr Kincaid asked.

Major Hunter just shook his head.

They found them lying close together. Nine elephants shot dead, their tusks sawn off, their corpses swollen in the heat and fly-infested. The Artists stood, horrified, sickened.

'Ivory poachers,' said Major Hunter. 'We're close enough to the border here. They cross over, butcher as many as they can, slip back over.'

'This is just sick,' said Dr Faustus.

Major Hunter shook his head. 'They don't look at it like that. One set of tusks sold on the black market will feed a family for a year. If they're caught, they know they'll be executed, but it's worth the risk.'

Dr Kincaid was well aware of ivory poaching. He had sponsored education programmes in the past and many poachers had been converted to gamekeepers over the years, but he knew that ultimately it was a losing battle. In the not too distant future, there might not be any elephants left for them to kill.

'Question is,' Mr Crown asked, 'if the poachers

come across our guys, what will they do?'

Major Hunter sucked on his bottom lip. He didn't need to answer.

'Exactly,' said Mr Crown. 'They won't want any witnesses. We need to get to our people now.'

Then they heard a shout of: 'Over here! Come over here!'

It was Bonsoir. They hurried across to where he was crouching down, partially hidden by a bunch of saw grass. He was shaking his head and looking at a baby elephant lying on its side, shot to death. Around one of the tiny little mounds where one day a tusk would have grown there was tied a red bandana.

'It's Katya's,' said Dr Kincaid.

Chapter Fifteen

Katya called a halt to the day's march and they began to search for shelter from the worst of the sun. They settled on the shade of a copse of trees. Before they sat down, Katya instructed them to cut and drag branches from thorn bushes, which they then formed into a tight circle around their camp. Michael didn't think a few branches would keep danger at bay until he tested one of the thorns with his thumb and blood immediately spurted out. Chastened, he lay down with the rest of them. But nobody was quite relaxed enough to sleep. The air was thick with the musty smell of wild animals, and despite Katya's confidence they were all dreadfully aware of how precarious their situation was. There was an odd kind of silence that came with the midday heat, but it was misleading. A savage death might only be moments away.

When it became clear that sleep was eluding them, Katya got them up and opened a gap in the perimeter. She sent Sam out with the gun to stand guard, and Jake and Pete to cut half a dozen long, straight branches from the trees above them.

'Spears,' said Katya, when they returned ten minutes later. 'We have one knife. Pass it around. Sheer off the twigs, sharpen one end.'

'Isn't it all a bit nineteenth century?' Pete asked.

'When we run out of bullets, or the gun jams, you'll appreciate having one.'

'If a lion charges at me, you think I'm going to throw a stick at it? I'm jumping into the nearest tree.'

'Not that many trees,' said Petra.

'And don't underestimate the speed of a lion,' said Katya. 'They look sleepy most of the time, but before you've run ten metres it'll have you down. One slice of its paw and your head will be off. Your best chance is to stand and fight.'

'How would you know?' Pete sneered. 'Did you read it in a book?'

Katya didn't even blink. 'Yes,' she said. 'And if a lion comes at me, and I have a book in my hand, I'll throw the book at it rather than run.'

'That's just ridiculous. Where are you going to get a book out here?'

He was hoping for a laugh. He didn't get one.

One minute a glowing red sunset, the next utter blackness. There was no moon, and the stars were at best hazy. Michael stood guard, the handgun on safety, and slipped it into the top of his trousers. He jumped when Katya suddenly appeared beside him.

'No sleep?' he asked.

'Dozed a little. You?'

'I'm on guard.'

'I know.' She smiled. 'Going to get them up now, get moving.'

'Don't the predators mostly hunt at night?' She nodded. 'Shouldn't we wait for daylight then?'

'Nope. We'll walk twice as far out of the heat.'

'But we won't be able to see where we're going.'

'We'll be fine. Within an hour our eyes will adjust to the darkness. We all have built in night vision, Michael, we just don't know how to use it.'

'Katya?'

'What?'

'You know an awful lot of stuff.'

'Not as much as I intend to.'

'Well, I'm glad you do.'

She hesitated, waiting for the inevitable barbed comment. But when nothing came she relaxed and said, 'I do what I do. You do what you do.'

'And what exactly is that?'

'Get us into more trouble, usually.' Again he was silent. She wasn't used to seeing him in such a contemplative mood. 'Michael. You're a survivor. You can't learn that. You were born with it. And if you're a survivor the people standing next to you have a better chance of surviving themselves.' She could just about see that he was nodding slowly. 'Now enough of the big thoughts and let's get these guys moving.'

'What if we accidentally leave Pete behind? He's the only one of them that's really sleeping.'

Katya looked towards the young Royal. 'Don't tempt me,' she said.

She was right, of course. Their eyes became used to the dark. It was not like looking down the night scope of an assault rifle, where you could pick out the whites of your enemies eyes at two hundred metres, but it was certainly good enough for them to cross country without stumbling over boulders or tumbling into hidden ravines. They had their single gun, their spears, a direction to march in and an ultimate goal. But they were still terrified. In their old camp, with tents, and fire, and Major Hunter theoretically watching over them, they had felt relatively safe. Now, marching towards the mountain, everything felt *alive*.

Ash summed it up: 'I don't like this,' he said, from his carefully chosen position right in the middle of the column. 'I really don't like this.'

'Nobody likes it,' said Jake.

'I can smell them,' said Ash. 'Lions. Tigers.'

'There are no tigers in Africa,' said Katya.

'They might be on holiday,' said Petra.

'I smell something,' said Ash.

'You smell yourself,' said Pete.

'Sing,' said Katya.

'What's that?' Michael called from the back.

'We should sing. If there's anything out there, noise will deter it.'

'What'll we sing?' Sam asked.

'What about the National Anthem?' Michael asked, mostly just for badness.

'*Bor-ing*,' said Pete.

They walked, they sang, they weren't attacked or eaten. Every kilometre or so Ash said he was hungry.

When he forgot to say it, they reminded him. It became a running joke. Black turned to grey, grey to blue. In the distance, the summit of Mount Zambella was for once not cloaked in cloud.

'Snow on top!' Michael called.

'Closer we get there'll be more vegetation, more fruit, berries, fresh water,' said Katya.

'How far do you think?'

'30km maybe.'

'Long way.'

'For a slacker,' said Katya.

By 10 a.m. the sun was starting to burn. Major Hunter had kept them walking through the worst of it because they'd had plenty of water to keep them hydrated, and even suncream to protect them. Now they had nothing. Katya was keeping her eye out for something as they progressed, and eventually her vigilance was rewarded. She let out a little yelp of excitement and darted off to their right. She'd spotted a clump of yellow flowers almost at ground level; but she ignored them and instead picked off half a dozen of the plant's thick, fleshy green leaves. She came back proudly displaying them to the little group.

Ash said, 'Can we eat them?'

'You can try.' She selected one of the leaves and split it down its spiny centre. A thick liquid oozed out. 'Meet *aloe succotrina*, or just plain old aloe to you and me. Mother nature's suncream, better than any factor fifty you'd pick up in the store.' She began to distribute the leaves amongst them. 'Cover yourselves. It'll buy us a few extra miles before we make camp.'

As they followed their instruction, Petra said, 'How come Major Hunter never showed us this?'

'Maybe he's on commission from the suncream company,' said Ash.

'Maybe he was an idiot,' said Pete, 'just like you.'

'Takes one to know one,' said Ash.

'Shut your face,' said Pete.

'Shut your own,' said Ash.

They were about to square up to each other when Sam distracted them by pointing up. 'Vultures!'

Half a dozen of them, high in the sky, wheeling around, perhaps two hundred metres away.

'They heard we were coming,' said Ash.

'You'll keep them well fed for about six months,' said Pete.

Ash ignored him.

Katya said, 'Who has the gun?'

Sam held it up. 'Why?'

'Might be an animal in distress. Fact that they haven't landed already means it could still be dangerous and they're waiting for it to die. Or something has killed it and is currently eating it. The vultures are waiting to pick over the bones. Either way – vigilance.'

'Interesting nature lesson,' said Pete, 'but can we just ignore them and keep walking towards the mountain?'

'You can if you want,' said Katya. 'Me? I intend to eat.'

'Eat?' said Ash.

'There's fresh meat up ahead. We need to pick up food where we can.'

'You mean like there's a McDonalds or something?' Pete asked sarcastically.

'She means to either kill what's dying up there,' said Petra, 'or chase off whatever's eating it.' She hesitated. 'Isn't that right?'

'That's the plan.'

Pete shook his head. 'If you think I'm eating some mouldy old maggot-ridden, putrefying dead thing, you're off your head.'

'Fine with me,' said Katya. 'Though I should point out that vultures are only attracted to fresh meat; if it's rotten they won't go near it. Good enough for vultures, good enough for us, that's what I say.'

Michael stepped up beside her. 'She may have somehow swallowed Google, but she does tend to know what she's talking about. I'm with Katya. Who else is?'

None of them looked exactly enthusiastic, but nevertheless they all raised their hands. Even, after a certain amount of prevarication, Pete.

Michael and Katya were on their bellies, peering through a gap they'd made at the edge of the long grass. There was a flat expanse of barren ground ahead of them; about forty metres away, two lionesses were greedily tearing at a zebra. Their muzzles were blood-soaked and the downed creature's entrails hung out of a massive gash in its side. Blood that had soaked out onto the parched ground had already dried hard and black. Satisfied with what they saw, the two young Artists backed away.

'OK,' said Katya as they rejoined the group, 'This is what we're going to do.'

When she explained the plan they all looked at her like she had a screw loose.

Jake put it into words. 'Katya, that's not a plan, that's a long suicide note.'

'It will work.'

'I'm not charging at a lion with a stick.'

'Two lions,' said Katya, 'and they're not sticks. They're spears.'

'They're sticks with pointy ends,' said Pete. 'And they're not that pointy.'

'It's not about how pointy they are,' said Katya, 'it's about the surprise element. We're not trying to kill them, we're trying to scare them off. Now are you with me or not?'

She looked around the group. Nobody met her gaze. Michael stepped up beside her.

'I don't understand you,' he said, looking at Ash, and then Jake, Sam, Pete and Petra. 'Just a few minutes ago we were all going to support Katya, and now the first time she asks you to do something you back down. What's with you?'

'A few minutes ago she wasn't asking us to attack a lion,' said Ash.

'Lions,' said Pete. 'With sticks!'

'For God's sake!' Michael erupted. 'We're fighting for survival out here, and if we don't do something to help ourselves, then one of those beasts out there is likely to help itself to one of us.'

'Can we not just shoot at them, scare them off?' Jake asked.

'Waste of a bullet,' said Sam.

'Exactly,' said Michael. 'We need to keep them until we *really* need them. Look – I think we need to do this. Yes, it's mad, and yes we could just pass on by. But it's about more than just blindly following what Katya says. All of us, we were sent on this trek, forced onto it. Even me. I don't even know what SOS is. I've been in trouble all my life. I burned my last school down because I didn't like it. And I hated this trek because I thought Major Hunter was an ass. Now I'm stuck out here in the middle of nowhere, and I'm hungry and I'm thirsty. But do you know something? I'm starting to love every minute of it. When I go home, and someone asks me what I did on my holidays, I'm not going to say I lay on a sun lounger and got a bit of a tan, I'm going to say I charged at a lion with a stick. They're going to give me some respect. Isn't that what we want? We're on the adventure of a lifetime, so let's bloody live it!'

Chapter Sixteen

One lioness was chewing Ash's leg. The other was up to her eyes in Jake's chest, at least until her eyes roved across the field of battle and spotted Michael, with a huge tear across his back, trying to crawl away even as the life ebbed out of him. The lioness roared, but didn't move. Instead she turned as her five cubs, until then hidden in the long grass behind her, jumped out, their sharp baby teeth glinting in the afternoon sun. The lioness raised one mighty, bloody, paw towards Michael and hissed, 'Feast my children, feast upon the human flesh!'

Michael reared up, panting and sweating and yelled 'No!' at the top of his voice.

Everyone fell about laughing at him.

He had dozed off, contented, stomach full, in the glow of a warm fire. They had reached the foothills of

Mount Zambella, walking through the full heat of the sun in their determination to get to water and the dream of cooler air. Pete, scouting ahead with the gun, had found a cave which, although it smelt heavily of animals and there were plenty of footprints of indeterminate origin in the fine red dust within, was nevertheless currently deserted. Without being instructed to they had found thorn bushes to barricade the entrance, and set a fire on which to cook the huge steaks they had somewhat squeamishly cut from the half-eaten corpse of the zebra.

Their charge, shouting and yelling, had worked *perfectly*. Ash, surprising himself and everyone else, sped ahead of the rest of them screaming like a maniac. The lions had been taken quickly by surprise and had bounded away before he or his comrades were anywhere near them. Michael actually had to grab hold of Ash to stop him pursuing them into the long grass on the other side of the barren ground. When he led him back to the zebra, the others were standing around it in disbelief that Katya's plan had actually worked.

'Did you *really* know that would work?' Petra asked.

Katya smiled bashfully. 'Of course. Sort of. Not really. I mean, not for certain. But I know humans have never been great hunters, even going back thousands of years. Early man used to survive on berries and what he could scavenge. The trick is to find an animal that *is* good at hunting – and let it do all the hard work.'

'Hey, Google,' said Pete, nodding at Katya, 'do you also know if eating this is going to kill us?'

'What's wrong, Pete, don't you trust me?'

'I don't trust anyone.'

'Right. Well, it doesn't smell rotten, and I don't see any maggots. So I guess it's fine.'

'You *guess?*'

Now three hours later, everyone fed, nobody sick, her guess had been spot on.

As he finished his third perfectly cooked zebra steak, Ash said, 'I'm seriously going to petition McDonalds to start doing zebra burgers. That was delish.'

It was colder now, but they enjoyed the freshness in the air. The vegetation was thicker, deeper, more luxurious thanks to the water running down off the mountain and spreading out through the foothills. The cave they had chosen was on a low hill covered with trees. They'd spotted baboons earlier jumping from branch to branch high above them, which Katya said was good news.

'If there's a predator, they'll soon let us know

about it; they can make a hell of a racket when they're spooked.'

Katya soon set about revving them up for another night walk. They were well fed and watered now, and inclined to relax for as long as they could, and it took her and Michael half an hour to get them all ready to move out. Their night vision was soon back in working order, which was a good thing, because the terrain was becoming increasingly difficult. The ground undulated, and the bushes and trees made it hard to see more than a few metres ahead; insects buzzed thickly around them as soon as they began to sweat; and every one of them lost their footing at some point and went rolling into the undergrowth. It was a miracle that none of them was seriously injured.

Michael was about to duck under a branch when he realized it was moving, and that there was no breeze to move it. He froze. He had been leading them in single file, so the others backed up behind him.

'What's—?' Petra began.

'Snake,' said Michael.

Everyone took a step back, apart from Michael. He was frozen to the spot.

Katya snapped up her flashlight. 'Puff adder,' she said.

'I don't need to know what it's called,' Michael hissed, 'I need to know if it will kill me.'

'Probably,' said Katya.

'What do I do?'

'Don't annoy it. Which might be difficult for you. And back away.'

He backed away. The adder slithered away along its branch.

Katya pushed past Michael to take up the lead. 'If we're going to stop every time you see a snake, we're going to get nowhere fast,' she said.

Michael was about to snap something after her when Pete pushed past him as well, and said, 'Chicken.'

As Petra moved past him she said, 'Next puff adder I find, it's going in his sleeping bag.'

Michael grinned and said, 'Wishful thinking. Having a sleeping bag, I mean.'

His legs now back in working order, Michael started walking again. Sam fell in beside him. She nodded towards Katya.

'Is it not very annoying,' she asked, 'having a girlfriend who knows everything?'

'She doesn't know everything,' said Michael. 'And she's not my girlfriend.'

Twenty metres later she said, 'I've seen the way she looks at you.'

'How does she look at me?'

'Like she's your girlfriend.'

'I don't think so. You're misreading her looks. When she looks at me she's thinking, that guy's an idiot.'

'You're not an idiot.'

'Well, I haven't taken any exams in it, but I've done all the course work.'

'You're funny. But you're no idiot. I've been watching you. Both of you. It's like you're joined at the hip. You arrived together. You stick up for each other. You both seem very well acquainted with this survival stuff. You said you were SOS when you arrived, then you said that was all bull this afternoon, now I'm inclined to think it's a double bluff and actually you are SOS.'

'SOS recruiting kids, yeah, *right*.'

'There's something going on.'

'If we were anything to do with SOS, we'd be doing a hell of a lot better than this.'

He could just about see that she was nodding in the darkness, and he wasn't sure if he was annoyed or relieved by it.

She said, 'Fair point. But there's something about her. She knows too much, she shouldn't be here.'

'I know what you mean,' said Michael. 'She is a bit of a control freak. Maybe that's her problem, she has to be in charge, she's like Hitler or—'

The walkers ahead of them stopped abruptly. Michael could make out Katya, crouching down, and waving behind her for them to follow suit.

'See what I mean?' Michael whispered to Sam.

She smiled as he moved past her, up to Katya. He knelt beside her and asked her what was up. She replied by sniffing up. Michael sniffed too.

'Smoke?'

Katya nodded. The others moved up beside them and dropped. They too detected the smell.

'Cooking,' said Ash. 'That means people, that means we're not lost any more, that means we're safe.'

He stood up. Michael pulled him down again.

'Could be anything, anyone,' said Katya. 'We scout it out. Come on, Michael.'

'Let me do it this time,' said Sam.

'You've been off on your own enough,' said Jake, 'I'll do it.'

'I haven't done any scouting yet,' said Petra. 'It has to be my turn.'

'Neither have I,' said Ash, 'give me the gun, I'll handle it no problem.'

Katya shook her head. 'No. Maybe the one person who hasn't volunteered should do it?'

They all looked at Pete, apart from Michael, who was studying his SOS partner. It was a risky suggestion. Yes, getting Pete to do it might be giving him some of the responsibility that this trek was supposed to instil in him – but sending him off by himself would also put him at risk, and the only reason they were on this journey was to protect him.

'Happy to oblige,' said Pete.

He reached for the handgun, but Katya held on to it.

'But—'

'Your job is to scout and report, not shoot.'

'But what if they attack me?'

'Run,' said Katya.

Pete shrugged and said, 'Whatever you say, *boss*.' He disappeared into the darkness.

They stayed where they were, assailed by mosquitoes and their own doubts; stopping seemed to re-enforce their fears in exactly the same way that their forward momentum had eased them.

'How long do we give him?' Ash whispered.

'What if he doesn't come back?' asked Sam.

'He'll be sitting there eating all the food before he

even thinks of us,' said Jake.

'He'll be back in some hotel having a bath and forget about us entirely,' said Petra.

'If he gets in trouble up there,' said Ash, 'all of his friends will rescue him.'

Nobody said anything, but they all tried to suppress their giggles.

They heard nothing for five minutes, then ten, then fifteen.

Then suddenly a cacophony of sound: people screaming and yelling, birds and animals screeching with fright – but above it all, the unmistakable rattle of automatic gunfire.

Chapter Seventeen

They ran, as panic stricken and out of control as the herd of elephants that had rampaged through their camp. Even Michael and Katya, who were supposed to be steady and logical in any difficult situation, were caught up in it. It had something to do with the wall of bullets zipping through the vegetation around them, the cries and yells and the snap of vegetation as unknown assailants raced towards them. It was about self preservation, survival and, of course, terror.

It was Michael who finally managed to stop their flight, and that was only by running faster than the others and heading them off. The shooting had stopped, the sounds of pursuit had faded.

Michael grabbed Sam as she ploughed through some bushes; he actually tripped Jake to prevent him disappearing; Petra stopped of her own accord; Katya actually backed into the small clearing, her eyes cutting into the darkness, ears pricked for trouble.

They flopped down, fighting for breath.

Katya suddenly snapped out, 'Ash, where's Ash?'

'Did they get him?' Petra asked.

'Who *are* they?' asked Jake.

'Did anyone see him?' asked Katya.

'I saw him,' said Sam, 'he was moving faster than I was.'

'I thought I was at the front,' said Michael, 'I was sure nobody was ahead of me . . .'

'Why did they start shooting?' Jake demanded.

'Maybe they'd met Pete before,' said Sam.

'This isn't funny,' said Katya.

'What're we going to do about Ash?' Petra asked.

'And Pete,' said Katya.

'And Pete,' agreed Michael.

He was their mission, and now he was gone.

They said nothing for fully thirty seconds, thinking through the possibilities. But then, from above, came the sound of someone clearing their throat. Sam snapped up the handgun.

'Don't shoot!' said Ash, halfway up a tree. 'It's only me!'

Michael put his hand over the gun and gently pushed Sam's hand down.

'How on earth did you get up there?' Katya asked. 'There aren't even any branches to climb up.'

'I don't know,' said Ash. 'I may need some help getting down.'

The others gathered around the base of the trunk, amazed by his speed and climbing skills, and quite happy to poke fun at him. Relief flooded through them, but once they'd ushered him down, it flooded straight out again.

'Like him or not, Pete's one of us,' said Michael. 'We have to find out if he's OK.'

'There had to be at least a dozen people chasing us,' said Sam, 'and they all seemed to be shooting. We have one handgun and some spears.'

'We don't know who they are or what Pete did to annoy them,' said Katya, 'but the possibilities are that he's dead, captive or he's run away.'

'Probably run away,' said Ash.

'Or sent them after us,' said Jake.

'Stop,' said Katya. 'This is serious. We have to find out. Yes, they have a numerical advantage, and they outgun us. Sure. But their pursuit lacked organization, and skill, and they were shooting wildly at targets they clearly couldn't see. They have no discipline, they are not an effective unit. We are.'

If Pete had been there, he would have said, 'Since when?'

But he would have been wrong, Michael knew it. Yes, they had fled the gunfire, but they had already proved that they could work as a team, they'd shown bravery in attacking the lions and resilience in putting up with Major Hunter's stringent regime and had even managed, until now, to survive perfectly well without him.

Going back for Pete would be dangerous, but not going back was unthinkable.

Gradually the frantic chatter of the baboons in the trees above quietened and the night assumed a windless calm. They sat where they were to discuss a plan, occasionally starting at a sudden cry or yelp or snort from the denizens of the jungle. Ironically, it was Pete's absence which allowed them to discuss their next step without disruption or dismissive or sarcastic comments. Michael and Katya both got a buzz out of them all working so well together. After about twenty minutes Ash raised his hand and said, 'I gotta pee.'

Michael said, 'Since when did you need permission?'

'OK, it's more than a pee. I think it may be the zebra coming back to haunt me.'

'Why do we need to know this?' Jake asked.

'Because I can pee over there,' he said, thumbing towards some long grass, 'but if I want to do . . . something else, I need to go a bit further.'

'Still too much information.'

'What I mean is, if I'm going that far I need some protection.'

'I'm not standing guard over you, if that's what you're saying,' said Petra.

Ash blew air out of his cheeks. 'I want the gun. Just in case.'

'No gun,' said Katya. 'Take your spear.'

'What if there's more than one of them?'

'Dig it out of the first guy's chest,' said Sam, 'then throw it again.'

'I'd really like the gun.'

'You could have done it by now!' Katya snapped impatiently. 'We're trying to decide something here, go do!'

Ash made a face, picked up his spear and ventured cautiously towards a clump of bushes. He stood behind them. He could still hear his comrades talking. He went a bit further. And a bit further. He didn't want them to hear him doing what he had to do.

Finally he was happy with his position. He

loosened his trousers and squatted down. He was actually surprisingly relaxed. He was quite good at compartmentalizing things. There were bad guys out there who had tried to kill them twenty minutes ago, but he was able to put that to one side while he concentrated on matters at hand. He began to think about movies, and how nobody ever went to the toilet in them. He couldn't ever remember seeing an action movie where the hero suddenly raised his hand and said, 'I need to do a number two.'

Ash's eyes shot up as a twig snapped somewhere in front of him. He held his breath.

Relax.

It's nothing.

You're used to this.

Another twig snapped. He was sure, or he was nearly sure he was sure, that something had just brushed past a low branch, and that he heard a slight twang as it rebounded into place.

It's nothing.

It's the breeze.

There is no breeze.

Ash swallowed.

Twigs and branches, that's all.

A baboon going for a late night swing.

Relax.

There.

All quiet.

But he wasn't relaxed, and certainly not enough to do what he had originally come for.

Another noise.

Something's moving.

No.

Yes . . .

A shape.

His heart was hammering. Ash eased up out of his squat and pulled up his trousers. He crouched again to pick up his spear. The shape was getting closer, and it had now assumed the outline of a man.

Oh my God, they're sneaking up on us, that's why it's been so quiet, they're going to ambush us and kill us all . . .

The man wasn't coming directly towards him. If he just stayed still the figure would move right past him.

But he couldn't just stand there.

The others would be taken by surprise, murdered while they sat discussing strategy.

He couldn't let it happen. He had been brave once already on this trek, leading the charge on the lionesses. He didn't know where that had come from, but now he had to call on it again. He had to face the enemy. Defend his comrades.

The best form of defence is attack.

He knew that.

The figure was about ten metres from him, to his left. In moments he would disappear back into the bushes and from there it was just a few metres to where Michael and Katya and Petra and Jake and Sam were sitting.

I have to save them.

Now!

Ash raised his spear and hurled it with all his strength.

The agonized scream shocked them all.

Michael was first to react. He snapped the gun out of Sam's belt and hissed, 'Stay here!' with such authority that none of them, not even Katya, thought about arguing with him. As he moved through them, Katya tossed him her flashlight and said, 'Be careful.' He nodded once and a moment later was swallowed up by the night.

He kept the torch off and secure in his back pocket, trusting in his night vision. He moved swiftly, the gun clasped in two hands and held out in front of him, roving from side to side. There was a whimpering sound coming from somewhere ahead. He moved to one side, fearing an ambush. Adrenaline coursed through him like electricity.

There.

One figure standing, another outline on the ground.

Michael fixed the gun on the one standing.

From the size and shape . . . it had to be Ash.

'Ash?'

No response.

'It's Michael.'

He took a step closer, gun centred, finger squeezing lightly on the trigger.

The figure turned. Ash spoke, his voice low, vague, shocked: 'What have I done?'

Michael moved right up beside him. 'You OK?'

'What have I *done*?!' Ash wailed.

The figure on the ground was groaning.

'It's OK, Ash,' said Michael, 'it's all right . . . you were just defending.'

Michael took one hand off his gun and eased the flashlight out of his pocket. He aimed the beam at the ground.

Michael swallowed. 'Or . . . on the other hand . . .'

He was looking at Pete Windsor.

Pete Windsor, the Prince, the young man who might one day ascend the throne of the United Kingdom of Great Britain and Northern Ireland, the Commonwealth. Whose head might be on a stamp.

Pete Windsor, with a spear jutting out of his side and blood seeping into the hard African dirt.

Chapter Eighteen

'He saw me . . . and he . . . did it on . . . purpose . . .'
Pete whispered, wincing as he agonizingly squeezed out
each word.

'I swear to God I didn't!' Ash was distraught.

Katya knelt beside Pete, examining the wound by
torchlight, her face grim.

'It was an accident,' she said, 'you know that . . .'

'He never . . . liked me . . . none of you do.'

'Shhhh, Pete . . . let me have a look.'

'How bad is it . . . Am I going to die . . . Please . . .
tell me . . . am I . . . ?'

'No, of course you're not. It looks worse than it is.'

'Get it . . . out of me . . . get it out . . .' Pete raised a
hand to tug at the spear jutting out of his side, but
Katya caught it.

'No, not yet, Pete. Just leave it for now.'

'I'm dying . . .'

'No, you're not.'

'I know I'm dying . . . I don't want to die out here. I want to go home . . .'

'Pete – I need you to be strong. Fight it. You'll be OK. You're part of our team, we need you.'

'You . . . don't need me . . . you've never . . . no one has ever . . .'

'Pete!' She crouched down right beside his ear, and began to whisper so that the others couldn't hear. 'Pete, listen to me. I know who you are, I know how important you are, what your destiny is. You're hurt, but we're going to look after you and get you home, OK? It's our job to do that.' He nodded vaguely. Katya sat up. 'You're *not dying*.'

Petra took her place, taking Pete by the hand and talking soothingly to him. He began to float in and out of consciousness. The others moved a few metres away and spoke in hushed voices.

'Well, doc,' Michael asked, 'what's the prognosis?'

'He's dying,' said Katya.

'Oh my God,' said Ash. 'I've killed him!'

'*Shhhhh!*' They all looked back at Pete. 'The spear has pierced his lung and collapsed it. He's bleeding internally and externally.'

'Shouldn't we, you know, pull the spear out at least?' Jake asked.

'Worst thing we could do. He'd bleed out. We've no bandages, no fluids, nothing to fight infection . . . unless we can get him to a hospital . . .'

'How long does he have?' Michael asked.

'Don't say that,' said Jake.

'I don't know. A few hours maybe.'

'OK,' said Michael.

'OK?' Sam cried. 'What do you mean OK? What's OK about it?'

'I didn't mean . . .' Even in the darkness he could see the tears in her eyes, shiny in the moonlight. 'I mean, OK, we're going to have to do something about it.'

'Like what?' Jake demanded. 'We've no way of doing . . . *anything*. We're just going to have to sit here and watch him die.'

'No,' said Michael. 'We're not.'

He turned and crossed back over to Pete. He knelt down opposite Petra.

'Pete . . . Pete?'

Pete's eyes were closed, his hair dank with sweat, his breathing laboured. He didn't respond.

Michael poked him.

'Don't!' Petra hissed. 'Let him rest.'

'No. It's important.' Michael poked him again. 'Pete? Pete? Pete?'

Pete's eyes flickered. 'Wha . . . ? Hey, Mike . . . Michael . . . did I ever . . . tell you . . . you're not . . . half as . . . tough as you think you . . .'

'No you didn't, Pete. Tell me later. Now you have to tell us what happened, back there, all the shooting?'

'It doesn't *matter*,' said Petra, 'just let him . . .'

'No, let him speak.' It was Katya, joining Michael. 'Pete?'

'You think . . . I did something bad . . . don't you? You're all against me, always have been . . .'

'Pete, concentrate. What happened when you scouted ahead? Why did they start shooting? Who are they?'

Pete managed to force a grim smile onto his face. 'It's your . . . worst nightmare . . .'

'What is Pete?'

'He's . . . he's still alive . . .'

'*Who*?'

'Major Hunter.'

By the time he'd finished, Pete's voice had been reduced to a dry rasp. His story jumped around all over the place, and twice he drifted off and had to be poked again so that they were sure to get all of the details. It wasn't just interest in what had happened to him – they had to know everything. It was, literally, a matter of life and death.

Pete had zeroed in on the source of the smoke quite easily. Before he'd gone very far he'd heard the sound of raised voices and crawled on towards them. He came upon a camp fire, with the body of a gazelle being cooked on a spit. A dozen men were gathered around it, drinking beer and, as far as he could tell, in the midst of an argument. They only quietened when they began to eat, cutting huge chunks from the antelope either with long knives or actually tearing them out with their hands and then swearing as they burned themselves in the process. To one side, and very close to where he lay hidden, Pete saw a large black tarpaulin, caked in mud and grass. There were reinforced grommets in the corners to which ropes had been attached so that it could be dragged along. Poking out from inside Pete could clearly see elephant tusks, dozens of them. Ivory poachers! Despite the fact that he and his companions were short of food and lost, he knew that these weren't the people to be seeking help from.

He was just on the point of making a quiet

withdrawal when one of the poachers tore off another chunk of meat and carried it across to the base of a tree; there was someone tied to it, sitting down and with his head slumped forward. The poacher gave the prone figure a kick and he looked up groggily. Pete's heart nearly stopped when he realized who it was: Major Hunter, indeed, but a much reduced version of their former leader. His face was battered and bruised, his sunglasses missing and his surprisingly small eyes looking terrified as he looked up at his captor's scowling face. The poacher barked something at him before pushing the meat into the Major's mouth, half choking him.

Pete lay in the grass, trying to decide on the best course of action. Go back for the others? Or try and help free the Major? He looked back to the fire, saw that the poachers were drinking again; their argument had resumed, and grown in intensity. A fight broke out; there was shouting and punching and kicking. It subsided. Then it started again. They were clearly a volatile bunch, and getting drunker by the minute. There might not be time to go for help.

As the poachers bickered, Pete moved around the camp and approached from the rear. He snuck forward, his progress masked by the trunk of the tree to which Major Hunter was secured.

'Major,' he whispered, 'it's me . . . Pete . . .'

'Pete! Oh, thank God!'

'Shhhh . . . I'll try and cut these ropes . . .'

'Yes, yes, cut . . . quick as you can . . . these guys are out of their heads . . .'

'Shhhhh . . .'

'Yes . . . but quickly . . .'

The poachers had used odd pieces of rope and various different strengths of vine to lash the Major to the trunk, it was difficult to cut through them with the only instruments Pete had at his disposal – his fingers and his teeth.

'They're taking me across the border, looking for a ransom . . . If they don't get it they'll cut my throat.'

'Shhhh, Major.'

'Hurry!'

The Major was panicking, straining against his bonds. He began to bang himself back against the trunk trying to loosen himself, but in fact only succeeded in loosening Pete's grip.

'Major . . . be *quiet*!'

And then suddenly there was a shout and someone jumped towards Pete, and Pete lashed out, his fist connecting with the man's jaw and sending him flying backwards, but yelling at the same time, loud enough for the others to stop their fighting and pick up their guns and come running. Pete had no choice but to flee, with Major Hunter screaming, 'Don't leave me! Don't leave me!'

The vegetation exploded all around as automatic gunfire zinged past his ears. It was a miracle that he wasn't killed. He ran and ran and ran, zigzagging, rolling, climbing and doing everything in his power to evade capture. They came so close. Twice they rushed past, narrowly missing him in the darkness.

A miracle indeed – right up to the point where he had been speared by his own side.

'I . . . didn't save the Major . . . I'm useless at . . .'

'You tried, Pete, it wasn't your fault.'

Pete closed his eyes.

Katya leaned closer. 'Pete . . . Pete . . . did you see any of them with a cell phone?'

But there was no response, he'd drifted away again.

Michael looked at Katya. 'Plan?'

'We have to go after them.'

Michael nodded.

'*What?*' said Jake.

'We have to save Major Hunter.'

'*Why?*' demanded Sam. 'Do you think he would come and save us?'

'It doesn't matter. It's the right thing to do.'

'The right thing to do is to get help for Pete.'

Katya took a deep breath. She looked at Michael. He gave a short nod. He had already given them one inspiring speech. It was her turn.

'You're right,' she said. 'Pete is our major concern – but the only way we're going to save him is by going back there. They're ivory poachers, the nearest border has to be about sixty, seventy kilometres away, they won't have come here by foot. My guess is their vehicles have either broken down or they were washed away in the same flash flood that caught us. They've dragged their ivory this far, but they aren't going to be able to drag it another seventy kilometres, even if there was a village nearby they're not just going to wander in with all that ivory and ask for help. They *must* have mobile phones. They *must* have called their paymasters and asked to be picked up. Maybe they've asked about a ransom for Major Hunter too. But right now one of those mobile phones is the only hope Pete has. We have to go back. We have to.'

Chapter Nineteen

The fire had just about gone out, but smoke continued to drift lazily upwards, mixing with the early morning mist that hugged the ivory poachers' camp. They were all still asleep, having drunk themselves into a stupor. Even the guard posted to keep watch on Major Hunter had succumbed. He had watched for more than an hour as the guard struggled to keep awake, his head lolling forward repeatedly, before finally giving up, lying down in the dirt with his rifle by his side, tantalisingly close.

The Major was in a bad way, filled with despair at the knowledge that he was most certainly going to be murdered. When he had first stumbled upon them, half delirious with exhaustion from his struggle to survive the flash flood, they had surrounded him and beaten him and threatened to kill him, and the only reason he was still alive was that he had promised to empty his bank account for them as soon as they crossed the border. He would in effect be paying his own ransom. And once they found out he had no money, having spent every last penny he owned to purchase the trekking business from the real Major Hunter, then they would without a doubt finish the job.

If he survived that long. He had a high temperature from an infection he'd picked up while trying to escape the river; he was dehydrated, he knew that; and he'd barely eaten. He wasn't even sure if one of his troop – was Pete his name? – had actually tried to free him during the night, or if he had imagined it his fever. Somehow he doubted that any of the kids had even survived the flood. They were a useless bunch, incapable of taking orders or completing the simplest task without whining about it. If they hadn't drowned, they had surely been shredded by lions or merely just starved to death wandering lost in the bush.

Major Hunter groaned. He was sweating despite the chill of the morning. Across the camp one of the poachers began to stir. He rolled over and began to pick at what was left of the antelope the poachers had sprayed with bullets the day before.

Major Hunter was an African legend – one of the last of the great white hunters.

Alger Hess, on the other hand, had never shot anything in his life.

And he was squeamish at the sight of blood.

He knew he was too exhausted to walk. They had already forced him to stumble along for miles, striking him with their gun butts to keep him moving. Where was the sense in making him feel worse to encourage him to move? When they cut his restrains in a short while and ordered him to march, he knew his legs would not work. So they would shoot him. He was certain. He closed his eyes tight and prayed.

When he opened them again twenty minutes later, Alger Hess thought he was having another dream. He imagined he could see one of his kids, Michael, the mouthy one, emerge from the trees and walk calmly into camp.

Couldn't be.

Alger squeezed his eyes shut, then opened them again.

The boy was still there. He was actually stepping over sleeping bodies. The poacher who had already woken emerged from bushes on the other side of the camp, having grunted his way through going to the toilet, and stood open mouthed, his automatic rifle hanging off his shoulder, as Michael calmly reached down and lifted a half empty bottle of the strong alcohol they'd been drinking the previous night, and in another rapid swoop plucked out one of the glowing embers from the fire.

The stunned poacher recovered his senses and shouted something, snapping the rifle up to his shoulder as he did.

Michael smiled and gave him the thumbs up.

The poacher was utterly confused. This wasn't how someone was supposed to react when you pointed a gun at them. All around the other poachers began to wake. Even as they turned, wondering what the disturbance was, Michael stepped back over them.

Alger couldn't believe what he was seeing. What was the stupid kid doing? The poacher was yelling again, the others were jumping to their feet and grabbing their rifles, yet Michael wasn't paying them any attention, neither surrendering as reason said he must, nor attempting to flee. In fact, he was standing over by the tarp, and now he was pouring the alcohol over it and brandishing the ember.

All of the poachers were up now, crowding around

shouting and yelling and threatening Michael, their weapons zeroed in on him, but nobody was prepared to take the first shot.

Michael raised his free hand. He looked calm. He looked confident. He said, 'Any of you guys speak English?'

The poachers looked at each other. One, a tall, skinny guy in a ripped yellow shirt said, 'I do . . . what you doing, man?'

'What am I doing? Is it not obvious? I'm going to set fire to your ivory.'

Yellow Shirt laughed nervously. 'We have many guns.'

'So do we.'

He lowered his hand. Immediately a shot rang out, biting into the dirt six inches short of Yellow Shirt's feet. He jumped back, but at the same time his rifle ranged to Michael's right, the direction from which the shot seemed to have come. The other poachers had all ducked down, with their guns pointing in the same direction.

'We don't want to kill you all,' said Michael, 'we want to bargain. We do not wish to destroy your ivory . . . we want to trade.'

Yellow Shirt moved his gun back on to Michael.

'One gun does not mean you can—'

Michael scratched lazily at his head. Another shot rang out, this time zinging into the dirt even closer to Yellow Shirt, but apparently from the opposite direction. Their guns moved towards its source . . . and then half of them moved back in the original direction. The poachers shouted amongst themselves, clearly confused.

'We will pick you off one by one,' said Michael. 'You are completely surrounded.'

'What . . . what do you want?' asked Yellow Shirt.

'We want your prisoner.' He nodded towards Major Hunter. 'And we want a cell phone.'

Yellow Shirt looked towards the Major. He swung his rifle round until it was aimed at him.

'You value him so much, what is to stop me shooting him?'

'Cos you will be the first person we kill if you do.'

Michael rubbed at his cheek. Immediately a third shot rang out, this time biting into the ground behind Yellow Shirt. Everyone swung in a new direction, this time off to the right.

The boy was right. They were surrounded.

Yellow Shirt nodded slowly.

'We do not doubt you are great fighters,' said

Michael, 'and if there is a fight, many on both sides will die. All we want is the prisoner and a phone. You get your ivory, and you get your lives.'

Again the poachers shouted loudly between themselves. Finally Yellow Shirt said, 'You take this man. He is worth much money. You leave ivory. But we have no cell phone.'

Michael felt his stomach lurch.

'They have one!' the Major shouted suddenly. 'I saw them use it . . . yesterday . . . they have one!'

Michael raised an eyebrow. 'Phone,' he said.

Yellow Shirt chewed on his lower lip. Then he looked at one of his comrades and gave a short nod. This poacher didn't look as if he was much older than Michael. He reached into his shirt pocket and produced a small, black phone. He showed it to Yellow Shirt, who nodded again, before tossing it to Michael, who caught it in one hand, and immediately slipped it into his pocket.

'OK, now the Major.'

Yellow Shirt himself produced a knife from his belt and strode towards their captive. He knelt down as if to slice through the material binding him to the tree, but instead pressed the point of the blade to the Major's throat. The Major could smell a rancid mix of rotting meat and congealed blood on it.

Yellow Shirt grinned back at Michael. 'We can harvest more ivory, but there is only one man.'

'Have it your way.'

Michael moved the ember over the alcohol soaked ivory. He lowered it to within an inch of the tarp.

One of the poachers yelled at Yellow Shirt. Another joined in, then a third. The true value of their prisoner was unknown, but they knew they would be losing a small fortune if the ivory went up in flames.

Yellow Shirt shouted something back. There was a further brief exchange before he snarled something and moved the knife from the Major's throat to the back of the tree and swiftly cut through the mix of rope and vine that had secured him through an arduous night.

Immediately the Major tumbled forward.

'Get up, Major!' shouted Michael.

'I can't! My legs . . .'

He was on all fours.

'Get up, or you get left behind. Now do it!' Michael barked.

The Major winced as he slowly rose. 'I'm not sure I can . . .'

'Start moving, you'll get blood back into them . . . Come on now . . .'

The Major laboured forward, slowly passing through the poachers to get to Michael. None of them moved for him. Two set their shoulders so that they crashed into him as he passed by, and he staggered first one way then the other, but miraculously he managed to stay on his feet. Finally he was beside Michael.

'Keep walking,' said Michael, and indicated the way he'd come.

'But . . .'

'Go!'

The Major lurched forward. Within ten metres he'd been swallowed up by the tall grass surrounding the campsite.

Every fibre of Michael's being was screaming at him to follow, but he couldn't. Not yet. He had to buy time. The Major would be moving slowly, and once Michael separated himself from the ivory, he would no longer have anything to bargain with. While the poachers were at the campsite they were exposed and could be pinned down, once they started their pursuit, which they surely would, there would be no way to cover them.

Particularly with just one hand gun.

It had been Katya's plan to position herself, Ash and Jake at different points around the poachers' camp, and to then have Sam race between those points with the gun, with each of them taking a shot at a pre-arranged hand signal from Michael. It was his job to cause enough of a delay between shots so that there was time to get the gun to the different firing positions and give the poachers the impression that they were surrounded – and it had worked perfectly.

But now they were in a stand-off. Michael counted to sixty in his head, even though he knew he was going too fast. It was probably only thirty seconds. Yellow Shirt was edging closer.

Go, go, go, go, go . . .

But still he stood his ground.

If everything was still going to plan, Sam, Jake and Petra would already have joined up with Major Hunter. Katya would be covering him with the gun, and Ash would be in position, ready to implement stage two of their escape. But it all depended on them getting the barely mobile Major sufficiently far away.

Yellow Shirt took another step closer. The other poachers moved as well. Their confidence was growing.

Time for another warning shot.

Michael pulled at his ear.

He waited for the shot to scare the poachers back again.

But it didn't come.

Maybe Katya missed the signal.

He pulled his ear again.

Nothing.

A thin smile spread across Yellow Shirt's face.

He's worked it out.

Michael frantically counted the bullets in his head. No, she couldn't have run out, there was a clip of twelve. And she wouldn't have run out on him. Katya loved nothing more than sticking to a good, clear plan. Something had gone wrong. Most likely the gun had jammed.

Now. Go.

'OK,' said Michael. 'You move any closer, and your head explodes.'

Yellow Shirt hesitated.

'We have our trade,' said Michael, 'now you all have a nice day.'

He backed away slowly towards the edge of the clearing. The poachers, almost as if working as one entity, took a step towards him.

Michael paused for just a moment. He looked at the ember still just about clinging to life in his hand. Then he tossed it through the air. Every single one of the poachers watched its trajectory as it sailed in a high arc and landed perfectly and magnificently on the alcohol-soaked tarp. Immediately it burst into flames.

There was yelling and screaming as the poachers charged forward trying to save their precious ivory.

All but Yellow Shirt. One glance told him that the precious ivory was ruined. He swung back to Michael – but he was just vanishing into the tall grass. Yellow Shirt let go with a sudden burst of gunfire, and was about to plunge into the grass after him when it too suddenly burst into flames, and he was forced to throw himself backwards in order to save himself.

As he lay on the ground, the fire rapidly spread through the tall grass, creating an impenetrable flaming curtain that surrounded them, trapping them in their camp while Michael rapidly caught up with a grinning Ash, deliriously happy at having put his expertise as an arsonist to good use by creating the flaming curtain using nothing more than a couple of rocks and some dried out elephant dung as flints and fuel.

The grass was bone dry and had ignited quickly. But it would also burn through fast – and then there would be nothing between the trekkers and the poachers.

They had a jammed gun and half a dozen spears, and were being forced to crawl along at a snail's pace by a man they all despised. They were being pursued by a dozen heavily armed poachers hell-bent on revenge.

The odds were not good.

Chapter Twenty

It was known as the tree of life.

But it was just as likely to become their tree of death.

It was their only hope. But if they were discovered, they would be trapped.

They had hoped for a longer window in which to flee from the poachers, but the ring of fire they had hoped would delay their pursuit had slowed them by only a few minutes.

The baobab was less than a mile from the poachers' camp. Katya had chosen it because its hollowed centre would provide shade from the sun for the young Royal and because she knew she would be able to tap into some of the hundreds of litres of water trapped in its trunk. It was only supposed to be a temporary refuge, somewhere to keep Pete safe while the operation to free

Major Hunter and gain access to a mobile phone took place, but now it had become their their final haven. They were all crammed in, praying that the poachers, scouring the undergrowth and the outer edges of the savannah, would not think to check there and would eventually give up their search and make for their homes across the border.

Ash and Michael had thundered through bushes, leapt over rocks and slid down short ravines in their attempt to lose their pursuers. They had fallen and rolled and tripped, but kept going. But the poachers were relentless. The boys had finally stumbled into the shelter of the baobab, hoping against hope that they hadn't left enough evidence of their passage for the poachers to track them directly to it.

Katya had cut an incision into the tree, and water was leaking out. She tore off the sleeve of her shirt, soaked it, and squeezed it into Pete's mouth. He had not spoken for a long time, and his breathing was as shallow as his brow was hot. She looked up at Michael, gave a slight shake of her head and said, 'Do it, do it now . . . we're running out of time.'

Michael reached into his pocket for the mobile phone. And shuddered. The screen was badly cracked.

He showed it to Katya. He took a deep breath and pressed the power button.

Nothing.

'Try it again!'

He tried it.

Nothing.

Michael exhaled. 'I fell trying to get away. It's useless!'

The others were looking at him. Their plan had worked almost perfectly, but it had ultimately been a complete waste of time. If by some miracle the poachers didn't find them, they would still be lost in the middle of nowhere with no hope of rescue. Pete was dying and there was nothing they could do now to save him.

Michael looked around them. 'I'm sorry . . .'

He wanted them to say it was OK, it was an accident, couldn't be helped, but they just stared desperately at him, their faces, their body language, everything screaming of despair and hopelessness.

Major Hunter, leaning back, his head lolling from side to side, muttered, 'This is all my fault.'

Michael was grateful that the focus shifted from him, at least for a few minutes. The Major was a sad sight. He had been so authoritative, scary, imperious behind his shades, but now he was a broken man. His power was gone. He looked smaller. His nose was dripping. His tiny eyes roved around them.

'I'm not . . . I'm not Major Hunter,' he said. 'Major Hunter is a great man . . . and I am . . . an accountant.'

'An *accountant*?' said Ash. 'But you . . . you trained as . . .'

'No . . . I'm just an accountant. My name is Alger . . . Alger Hess. I just always dreamed of . . . being a great hunter. Like him . . . Major Hunter . . . and then I . . . I won the lottery . . . not, not, not millions, but enough to buy . . . and I thought I knew it all from, you know . . . reading books and watching . . . documentaries.'

'Documentaries!' Sam exploded. 'You mean we were following you and all you knew was what you saw on the television?'

'Yes! I'm sorry! I thought it would be easy to apply what I saw to . . . to real life . . . and I thought it was working . . . just common sense. But then . . . then it all fell apart. I'm sorry. I led you into this. I just wanted to . . . I just wanted to *be* someone important.'

Michael crouched beside him. 'I don't believe you. I saw you wrestle with a lion. Accountants don't wrestle with lions.'

Alger shook his head sadly. 'It was all a set up. The lion belonged to one of the truck drivers, he'd had it since it was a cub, raised it. It's a pet, it was used to playing with humans. I knew one of you would be watching me, it was just a ploy to make you . . . fear me. I'm sorry.'

They stood, open mouthed in disbelief, for the moment forgetting their dire situation.

'I'll tell you one thing,' said Jake, 'I'm never telling anyone that I followed an accountant into the jungle. They'd never let me forget it.'

'Me neither,' said Petra.

They were still looking at him when a weak voice came from behind.

'Plonker.'

They turned in time to see Pete's eyes flutter briefly and close. Katya hurried to him and knelt down. He was still breathing. But only just. Michael couldn't help but admire him keeping up his Cockney act right to the end.

'Let me look at the phone,' said Jake, 'maybe there's some way I can . . .'

Michael showed it to him, but shook his head at the same time. 'There's no way, the SIM's nearly bent in half. Even if we had . . .'

'Shhhhhhh . . .'

It was Samantha, a finger to her lips, her eyes wide with panic.

Michael strained to hear.

Yes.

Voices.

They weren't loud, and it was a miracle that Sam had picked up on them. Their footfalls were light, cautious and very, very close.

They all held their breath. Katya had sent Petra and Ash out with a leafy branch each to wipe away any footprints on the dusty ground approaching the tree, but that would only provide the flimsiest protection. If the poachers were following their tracks, then they led to this exact area, but didn't go anywhere. They had to be *here*.

But they couldn't quite work it out.

There were several baobab trees within a few dozen metres, and the poachers looked up into their high branches, thinking that that must be the explanation. But there was nobody there. Previous generations would have known about the baobab and its almost magical qualities, but these poachers had lived all their lives in ramshackle villages, prisoners of poverty without any of the old wisdom. Now, confused, they began to murmur amongst themselves. They had given pursuit, but now they were growing concerned. They wanted to start their journey home, get across the border where they would be safe from the game wardens and the possibility of arrest and execution. They began to retrace their steps. Of them all, only Yellow Shirt stayed where he was, standing still, listening, ignoring his comrades' entreaties to follow.

Inside the tree, they hoped against hope. They could just about tell that the poachers were moving away, but they were blind, they couldn't know that Yellow Shirt was still there.

And then, just as surely as he had led them into this mess, Alger Hess led them a little further down the path of doom.

He sneezed.

Not loud.

But loud enough.

A grin spread across Yellow Shirt's face. He shouted after his comrades, pointing excitedly at their baobab. They ran back, no need for stealth. Their prey was trapped. They would soon be free to go home without any fear of being exposed as poachers.

All they had to do was execute the witnesses.

They lined up.

A dozen automatic rifles all pointed at the tree.

And soon the air was thick with gun smoke and filled with the sounds of screaming.

Chapter Twenty-One

They couldn't help themselves.

They screamed as they dug their faces into the hard packed mud at the base of the hollow baobab, lying as flat as they could as bullets peppered the trunk and the air filled with thousands of splinters. Katya's hand found Michael's and squeezed. Sam had her arm round Ash. Ash had his arm round Petra who had thrown herself on top of Pete to protect him. At the very last moment, Jake had hauled Alger Hess down to ground level because he seemed incapable of doing it himself. There was that single unbearably loud volley from the ivory poachers, and then a short pause before it erupted again.

The only difference this time was that there was a curious kind of calm within the tree. The rain of splinters continued, for sure, but they were the lighter ones, floating calmly down. The walls of the baobab showed at least a hundred holes from the first attack, sunlight bursting through them like searchlights in a fog, but there were no new ones. The shooting was continuing, but it wasn't at their tree any more.

They can't decide which one we're hiding in. They're shooting them all up.

Still, Michael knew it was only a matter of time.

The trees were hollow.

They had been able to climb inside. The poachers would just as easily be able to check if they had succeeding in their massacre. Katya, equally puzzled by their unexpected stay in execution, began to raise her head. Michael pushed it down again.

The firing stopped.

There were footfalls outside their tree.

Then *on* the trunk.

Someone was climbing.

This is it then.

Katya's hand squeezed his ever harder.

Michael tried desperately to have a pleasant final thought.

But the only one that would come was: *This is going to be really painful.*

Then: *Get on with it.*

And when it didn't come, he opened one eye, then the other, and blinked up through the swirling dust and piercing sunlight at a familiar face gazing down.

'What the bloody hell are you hiding in a tree for?' Bailey asked.

They emerged slowly, blinking into the brightness.

The real Major Hunter had led the attack side by side with Mr Crown and with the other Artists only a few steps behind. They had swept across the short expanse of open ground so quickly and with such stealth that they had taken the poachers completely by surprise. Every one of them now lay in the dirt, disarmed, their wrists and feet bound.

One by one, the trekkers were helped from the tree, until only Michael and Katya remained, kneeling beside Pete. Bailey made way for Dr Faustus, who climbed in to examine Pete. The grim set of his face told them everything they needed to know.

'I did what I could,' said Katya. 'We had nothing . . . I couldn't—'

'It's OK,' said Dr Faustus.

'But I'm trained, if I could only have gotten hold of—'

She was on the verge of tears.

'You did everything you could. Now I need some space. And some muscle.'

Michael and Katya climbed out of the baobab, allowing Mr Crown and Major Hunter to take their place and use their strength to help manoeuvre Pete up and out. Sam, Petra, Jake and Ash were jubilant at having survived and the prospect of a swift exit from their calamitous trip into the African savannah. They were going home. But neither Michael or Katya felt like joining in their celebration. They were almost as downcast as Alger Hess, who was sitting on his haunches, staring at nothing.

Bonsoir came up. 'Hey, you guys OK?'

Michael just shook his head.

Katya said, 'This has been a disaster from start to finish.'

'How so? Aren't you alive? Hiding in a baobab, stroke of genius? Setting fire to the grass to attract our attention? Brilliant.'

'We failed in our mission,' said Katya. 'Pete Windsor has a spear sticking out of him. Even Doc Faustus isn't sure if he'll survive. We didn't protect him.'

Bonsoir nodded grimly.

But there was something about the way he did it that

Michael didn't understand. There was kind of a sparkle in his eye.

'What?' Michael demanded bluntly.

Bonsoir cleared his throat. 'The spear is unfortunate. But . . .'

Katya's brow furrowed. '*What?*'

'Maybe you should talk to the boss.' Bonsoir looked across at Dr Kincaid, who was busy talking to Dr Faustus as he knelt beside Pete. He had already given him several injections and attached a line for fluids. The boy's eyes were open, but unfocussed.

Michael and Katya waited impatiently for Dr Kincaid to finish. When he did, he turned to them and saw the expectant look on their faces.

'*What?*'

'What haven't you told us?' Katya demanded.

Dr Kincaid was clearly doing his best to stop a smile from appearing.

'About what?'

'You know what we're talking about!' snapped Katya.

Dr Kincaid pretended to look puzzled. 'Me . . . ? Oh . . . *right*. Yes. There was something.'

'*What?*' Michael demanded.

Dr Kincaid cleared his throat theatrically. 'Well, do you know the way you're both relatively new to the

Artists? And you know that while we trust you implicitly, you're still under training, right?'

'*Yes*,' said Katya, teeth gritted.

'I, we, felt it was important, helpful, and quite, ahm, reasonable to withhold certain information. It was important that our young Royal didn't suspect that you were Artists, and that you weren't seen to be giving out any special treatment.'

'We *didn't*,' said Michael.

'We were *extremely* careful,' said Katya.

'And that's good. But we needed to be certain.'

Katya shook her head. 'I don't understand. We did everything we could to protect him, and we didn't give ourselves away, not until the very, very end. He was delirious anyway, he probably doesn't remember.'

'Yes, well,' said Dr Kincaid. 'The problem is, he is actually a she.'

Their brows furrowed instantaneously. And they spoke as one: '*What*?'

'Ahm, yes. You see, Pete Windsor . . . The fact is, *that* young man isn't actually a Royal at all. He's just plain Pete Wilson, an East End boy with a bit of an attitude problem.'

'But . . . but . . . but . . .'

Katya just couldn't compute it.

'You see,' Dr Kincaid continued, 'all this time you've actually been in the presence of Her Royal Highness, Lady Samantha Windsor. She's actually about twelfth in line to the throne, but she's been in all kinds of trouble, and it was becoming increasingly difficult to cover up the mayhem she's been causing. They sent her on this trip as a last resort. Do you think it worked?'

Michael was too busy glaring down at Pete to answer. 'He's . . . he's . . . he's . . . ?'

Pete mumbled something, but it was indistinct.

Michael moved a little closer. 'What was that?'

'Plonker,' rasped Pete.

Michael spun away, furious, only to find Samantha standing right behind him.

'*Lady* Samantha?' Michael growled.

She smiled broadly. 'Absolutely. But you can still call me Sam. After you bow.'

National Park Rangers arrived in a small fleet of Land Rovers to take the poachers away. Pete was loaded onto the helicopter and secured. The senior Artists boarded and Mr Crown was poised in the doorway to haul up the young trekkers and Alger Hess. Nobody had said much to the fake Major Hunter, apart from Major

Hunter himself, who had yelled at him and tried to punch his head off. Mr Crown, Bonsoir and Dr Faustus had had to use their combined strengths to restrain him.

Now Michael stood with Lady Samantha, Katya, Jake, Ash and Petra, with a miserable looking Alger Hess a little off to one side. Mr Crown raised his hand and indicated for them to approach.

As Michael was about to step forward, Katya suddenly said, 'No.'

'*No?*'

'We can't. We can't go.'

'What are you *talking* about? We have to get Pete to hospital.'

'They can get Pete to hospital. We don't need to go with him.'

Mr Crown was waving with increasing impatience.

Katya shook her head. 'Listen to me, all of you. We came out here to do something. Climb to the top of that mountain. We need to finish the job.'

'*What?*' said Ash. 'Are you mental or something?'

'I may be. But you all came on this trek to learn something. I don't know if you have. I don't know if you'll be different when you go home. But I do know we're a good team, we work well together. And I think maybe you won't want to go home thinking you didn't finish what you set out to do.'

'You *are* mental,' said Ash.

'Will you get on board!' Mr Crown yelled above the sound of the blades, now beginning to rotate with increasing speed.

Michael laughed suddenly. He could suddenly see the logic in it. 'We've survived this far. We've battled lions and poachers and elephants and rivers, what've we got to be afraid of?'

'You're *both* mentalists,' said Ash.

But Lady Samantha was smiling. 'I wouldn't want to go home thinking the mountain beat me,' she said.

'We've no equipment, no supplies,' said Jake.

'There'll be some on the chopper, the rest . . . we just use our initiative. Scavenge, build, live off the land.'

'The land nearly killed us!' wailed Ash.

'I think we could do it,' said Petra. 'And a couple more days aren't going to kill us. Unless of course, they do.'

Katya nodded from Michael to Sam to Petra to Jake. They were all, inexplicably, smiling.

'One more thing,' said Katya.

Ash groaned.

'I think Major Hunter should lead us.' She turned

and looked at the miserable specimen they hadn't yet properly begun to think of as Alger Hess. '*Our* Major Hunter.'

'What on earth are you talking about!' Ash roared. 'He's a bully, he's a sadist, he knows nothing about survival, he can hardly walk and he's a . . . he's a . . . he's an accountant for God's sake!'

'I know,' said Katya. 'And he's out here for exactly the same reason you all are. To re-invent himself. He's made a lot of mistakes, but maybe everyone needs a second chance to sort their lives out.'

They had no answer to that.

Even Michael. He thought the idea was nuts, but there was still something undeniably *right* about it. He had hated the Major with a passion, but this man was no longer the Major. He was just an ordinary, ordinary man who had let his dreams run away with him.

'Hey, Major, what do you think?' Michael asked.

Alger Hess looked up, still dazed. 'Wh . . . what?'

'Do you fancy leading us up Mount Zambella?'

Confusion swept across his face. 'What? Mount . . . are you serious?'

'Yep,' said Katya. 'We're serious.'

Alger cleared his throat. 'Would . . . would I get paid extra?' Before anyone could snap anything, he held up his hands. 'I . . . I would be delighted!'

'Has the entire world gone crazy?' Ash asked.

They all looked at him.

'Probably,' said Michael. 'So – you coming with us, Ash?'

Ash blew air out of his cheeks. He glanced back at the helicopter. In a few hours he could be back in a nice hotel, eating a large meal, recovering from the deprivations of his time on the savannah. His mouth was already watering.

But then he let out a loud sigh. 'I think you're all as mad as a bag of spiders, but I'm not going to be the only one who doesn't finish the trek. Count me in.'

The rotation of the chopper blades was almost unbearably loud now, and it was beginning to hover a little above the ground. Mr Crown remained in the doorway beckoning furiously and screaming at them to get on board, but his voice was lost in the racket.

'Right,' said Katya, 'that's all agreed then. Now who's going to tell Mr Crown?'

'You,' grinned Michael, pushing her forward.

*Relive Michael and Katya's adventures in the
thrilling first* SOS Adventure *story:*
ICEQUAKE

Read on for the first chapter . . .

Icequake

The hunter had paid fifty thousand dollars to kill a polar bear – and he wasn't going home without one.

They'd been out from Miller's Harbour for three frustrating days, without even the hint of a bear. But at last they had picked up the trail early that morning and were now preparing to move in for the kill.

Pretty soon the skin would be hanging on the wall of his den back in Milwaukee, and all his pals who went out shooting harmless creatures like rabbits or deer would be green with envy. They would know that he'd taken on the mightiest carnivore on God's earth and defeated it.

Usually he was an accountant. He lived in the suburbs, he wore a boring grey suit, and the most exciting part of his day was getting on a train in the morning. He wasn't fabulously wealthy, but he was rich, and like many rich people he was very, very bored.

But not on this day.

If his friends could see him now, standing on the ice plain, the temperature minus thirty, all kitted out in his fur-trimmed parka, his face mask and tinted goggles, his binoculars hanging around his neck, the huskies barking around him, they would be jealous as hell – particularly when they saw him raise his rifle and scan the horizon. Not just any rifle, either. It was a .300 Winchester Magnum, the kind snipers used in the army, accurate to 1100 metres.

For this one day out of his whole life, John Gordon Liddy III was a man of action.

It would also be the day he died.

Liddy and his Inuit guide, Paul Nappaaluk, had been tracking the bear for about an hour. Liddy's excitement was visibly growing, but it was hard to tell with Paul. He was a small, weather-beaten man, and he didn't say much, didn't react to anything. Liddy could hardly even guess his age – maybe somewhere between sixty and seventy, perhaps even eighty. He wasn't like any old man Liddy had ever met. He was as tough as nails, and drove them relentlessly. At first Liddy had attempted to keep pace with him, but before very long he had collapsed down on to the sledge and allowed the dogs to carry him as well as their supplies.

Liddy had paid not just to kill the polar bear, but to enjoy the whole 'Eskimo' experience. He knew he wasn't supposed to call them Eskimos, but he could hardly help himself. Hadn't he grown up reading all about them? So far, however, he wasn't too impressed. The blubbery food Paul cooked was so revolting he'd given it to the dogs. In the dark of his tent, he'd chomped on a Power Bar and dreamed about McDonald's chicken nuggets. He was freezing, and hungry, and absolutely exhausted, and he missed having a television and a cell phone and doughnuts, but getting the bear would make it all worthwhile.

Sleep was impossible, with the wind howling and the yelping dogs. One of them had tried to bite a lump out of him when he'd gone for a pee. He had found Paul already standing outside, with his rifle raised to his shoulder.

'Something wrong?' Liddy had asked.

'Something spooked them,' said Paul.

Liddy just grunted and concentrated on trying to pee. It was so cold he was worried about *it* freezing up and dropping off. He washed his hands with snow and tramped back to the tent. He was paying far too much money to worry. The old man could stay on guard all night. Paul had the same rifle he had; there wasn't a creature on the planet could stand up to a Winchester Magnum. Besides, Paul was probably just playing it up, making like there was something out there. It was all part of the 'experience'.

But if those dogs don't quit hollering, I'll shoot one of them myself.

He wasn't an *entirely* unpleasant man, John Gordon Liddy III. He was just spoiled by civilization. If he had wanted to prove how brave he was to his friends, there were easier things he could have done, but no, here he was, on top of the world, a hundred miles from the nearest outpost and mere hours from death.

It was a little after noon when they saw the bear, about 1500 metres ahead, and facing away from them, halfway up a short incline. Paul raised his binoculars. Liddy preferred to study the beast through the telescopic sights of his rifle. His finger was already curling around the trigger. But he didn't shoot. The bear was still too far away, and he wanted the satisfaction of being close; he wanted to be able to look into the whites of his eyes as he killed him.

They left the dogs with the sledge, and moved cautiously forward. The bear was pawing at the snow, digging for something, its back to them, blissfully unaware that death was approaching – at least until the dogs behind them suddenly began to yelp again, probably having caught its scent. The bear turned slowly, its nose in the air. They were perhaps two hundred metres away. Liddy walked with his rifle to his shoulder and the creature in his sights, and now everything was perfect. He would have gone for a head shot, but he didn't want to spoil the look of the trophy he would soon have hanging on a wall at home. He was going to shoot it right in the heart.

Liddy began to squeeze the trigger, but just as he applied the final, killing pressure, Paul suddenly forced his barrel down. Liddy turned angrily to the Inuit. The old man was pointing to the left of the bear.

Liddy peered into the whiteness. At first he couldn't see anything. In truth he was finding it hard to take his eyes off the bear, which was now raised on its hindquarters, staring at them. Behind them the dogs continued to yelp and bark. But then he saw two disparate spots of movement. He raised his binoculars.

Cubs.

Two cute little balls of fur, frolicking in the snow, close to their den.

'We can't shoot her, Mr Liddy.'

'I got a licence, and I'm gonna shoot me a bear!'

'No, sir, terms of the licence forbids—'

'I don't care. I've come this far. I'm not going to walk away!'

Liddy snapped the rifle back to his shoulder and pulled the trigger. There was a loud crack. But he missed. Liddy had jerked at the trigger instead of gently squeezing, and the bullet had flown wide of its target.

'God damn it!'

Paul made another grab for the rifle, but Liddy threw him off. The old man tumbled away.

The bear had gathered the cubs to her now and was trying to shepherd them over the brow of the hill, but they thought it was just another game and tried to squeeze out of her grasp.

Liddy knew then that he would kill the cubs as well. He would have a whole family on his wall. He began to squeeze the trigger, but he hesitated at a noise from behind, some kind of snorting and growling.

One of the dogs must have gotten loose.

But then John Gordon Liddy III was hurled to the ground. He didn't even have time to scream as the huge creature pounced on him and sank its teeth into his throat and ripped the life from him.

Paul, thrown to one side by Liddy, had been separated from his rifle, and now it lay off to one side, on the far side of the creature. Its giant head turned towards him, it rose to its full height and it roared.

It was a polar bear, but fully twice the size of any he had ever seen.

Its jaw was a mass of sharp teeth, its muzzle soaked in blood.

All Paul's years of experience, and he hadn't realized that while they were hunting one creature, another was hunting them. A bear that had stepped out of the myths he had heard around the camp fire as a boy.

And now it was coming for him.